W9-BBQ-127

Also by Jamie Blair

Leap of Faith
Lost to Me
Deadly Dog Days

CANAL DAYS
Calamity

A Dog Days
MYSTERY

JAMIE M. BLAIR

MIDNIGHT INK
WOODBURY, MINNESOTA

MIDNIGHT
INK

FIRST EDITION
First Printing, 2017

Book format by Cassie Kanzenbach
Cover design by Ellen Lawson
Cover illustration by Ben Perini
Editing by Nicole Nugent

Midnight Ink, an imprint of Llewellyn Worldwide Ltd.

This is a work of fiction. Names, characters, places, and incidents are either the product of the author's imagination or are used fictitiously, and any resemblance to actual persons, living or dead, business establishments, events, or locales is entirely coincidental.

Library of Congress Cataloging-in-Publication Data
Names: Blair, Jamie M., author.
Title: Canal Days calamity / Jamie Blair.
Description: First edition. | Woodbury, Minnesota : Midnight Ink, [2017] |
  Series: A dog days mystery ; 2
Identifiers: LCCN 2017005421 (print) | LCCN 2017011865 (ebook) | ISBN
  9780738753072 () | ISBN 9780738751221 (softcover : acid-free paper)
Subjects: LCSH: Murder—Investigation—Fiction. | City and town
  life—Fiction. | GSAFD: Mystery fiction.
Classification: LCC PS3602.L3348 (ebook) | LCC PS3602.L3348 C36 2017 (print)
  | DDC 813/.6—dc23
LC record available at https://lccn.loc.gov/2017005421

Midnight Ink
Llewellyn Worldwide Ltd.
2143 Wooddale Drive
Woodbury, MN 55125-2989
www.midnightinkbooks.com

Printed in the United States of America

To Claudia and Ethan

ACKNOWLEDGMENTS

I'd like to thank cozy mystery readers and writers, who champion amateur sleuths big and small, like Agatha Raisin, Hannah Swensen, and my own Cameron Cripps-Hayman. Cameron and I are both grateful to Rebecca Friedman, Terri Bichoff, and Nicole Nugent for making it possible to share the Dog Days Mysteries with you. And a big thank you to my daughter, Claudia, for naming Colby and Jack!

· One ·

*C*anal Days would be the death of me if polka dots didn't kill me first.

"Mrs. Nelson!" My sister, Monica, shouted, chasing the eldest of Metamora's matriarchs around the outside of Dog Diggity. Letting the spry ninety-three year old woman—although, she claimed to be twenty-three since she was born in a leap year—loose with a paint brush was a recipe for disaster. Elaina Nelson was obsessed with polka dots and determined to place her trademark dots all over the exterior of the brick building. Since she owned the property, Monica had agreed to partner with the eccentric old woman in opening her dog treat business.

Elaina's shop, Nelson's Knitting Needles, had been less of an actual store and more a place where Elaina stored and stocked knitting supplies, which she gave away to her friends. When Monica approached her about leasing the shop for Dog Diggity, Elaina had been more than eager to let her move in—for *free*—with the stipulation that she got to be a part of the business.

We watched Elaina disappear around the corner behind the building. Monica picked up the pace, going from jog to full-out run to catch up with the old lady. I only ran if being chased by dogs.

"Mrs. Nelson!" Monica called again, rounding the corner after her.

As soon as my sister was out of sight, she let out an ear-splitting scream. My heart jolted in my chest. Adrenaline kicked in, and before I knew it, my feet had taken me behind the building.

"Don't touch him!" Monica yelled.

"Oh, good gravy," I said, taking in Elaina standing over a man lying prone on a bench beside the back door, her paint brush raised above him, a bright red splotch on the back of his shirt.

"Good Luck Chuck ran out of luck!" she said, laughing like a loon. The old woman made sense about 20 percent of the time. The other 80 percent of what she uttered was up to interpretation.

"Come on, Mrs. Nelson," I said, hooking my arm with hers. "Let's not paint the outside of the building or the bums sleeping behind it."

I ushered her away. Monica stood frozen in place with her hands over her mouth, eyes wide, staring at the man on the bench.

"Mon? You coming?" I asked.

"He's not breathing," she whispered. "I don't think that's paint, Cam."

"What?" I spun around and took another look. Come to think of it, I'd never seen a bum in the four years I'd lived in Metamora. "Who is he? You don't think…"

Monica nodded. "See if he has a pulse."

"Me? Why me?" I was more than reluctant to approach the man. Four months ago I'd discovered the body of one of our neighbors submerged in the canal. I wasn't eager to find another.

"He's gone," Mrs. Nelson said. "God rest his soul." She made the sign of the cross, like a priest in white patent leather sneakers with hair died the color of cherry licorice.

Monica let out a whimper and I gave in, dropping Elaina's arm. My extremities went cold and numb as I slowly approached the man on the bench. How was this happening again? He couldn't be dead. The odds were against it. If he was, I was officially the unluckiest person on the planet. Well, the dead man would be more unlucky than me, I supposed.

I reached out, averting my eyes from the red blotch on his back. My hand shook. My fingertips touched the side of his neck. His skin was cool despite the unnaturally warm temperature for the end of October. There was no pulse to be found. I took a deep breath and shifted my gaze to the spot on his back. There was an entrance wound from what I assumed was a bullet. The red substance surrounding it was definitely not paint. It was blood.

"He's gone," I said. "He's been shot."

Monica gasped and whimpered again. Mrs. Nelson clucked her tongue and said, "Poor Chuck."

"Monica, get Mrs. Nelson out of here. I'm calling 911."

She shook her head, bringing herself out of her stupor, and took Elaina by the arm. "Let's go up front, Mrs. Nelson."

I dug into my handbag. After always having to sift through a ton of junk to find what I was looking for, I'd downsized. Unfortunately, in my effort to become more organized, I'd picked a bag with what seemed like a thousand pockets. Zippers and snaps hid away all that was left inside to contend with.

The first pocket I searched contained a rectangular mirror, not my cell phone. The second turned out to hold a pad of Post-It notes. How many rectangular objects did I have stuffed inside this thing, anyway? I unzipped a third pocket to find a box of gummy bears. "You have got to be kidding me." Just short of tearing the bag apart, I finally unearthed my phone and jabbed the keys for 911.

I reported my emergency and made my way to the front of Dog Diggity just in time for my husband, Ben—from whom I was currently separated, but dating—to park his big police pickup truck, Metamora One, in front of the building.

"Hello, Mrs. Nelson," he said. "Monica. Cam."

"You're fast!" Mrs. Nelson said. "Like Superman!"

"Fast?" Ben asked, his brow creasing as he took in the expressions on my and Monica's faces.

"What's going on?" he asked, just as his police radio went off. "Dispatch to Metamora One. Come in Metamora One."

Ben reached into his pickup's cab and answered the call. "Metamora One. Go ahead."

"Report of a 10-54 at Dog Diggity. Proceed to location immediately for assistance."

"10-4."

He spun around and looked at me through thunderous eyes. "Cameron, please tell me you haven't stumbled on another body."

"It's not my fault! Mrs. Nelson found him. I only called it in this time."

"Stay here," he ordered the three of us, and trooped behind the building to check out the crime scene.

What seemed like only ten seconds later, he'd radioed for back-up and sirens blared down the alleyway beside the canal toward us. In a town as small as Metamora, sirens were a call to action, and everyone came running. Soapy Thompson—whose real name was Pete—the mayor and owner of the Soapy Savant, was the first of our neighbors to come to our aid.

"Do you know who it is?" he asked after we'd relayed the tragedy.

"Poor Chuck," Elaina said once again.

"We don't know," Monica told him, "but Mrs. Nelson seems to think his name is Chuck."

"I don't know anyone named Chuck in town," Soapy mused, stroking his white beard.

Sue Nelson, Elaina's granddaughter and owner of the Soda Pop Shop, came running up next. "Are you okay?" she asked, eyes creased with worry.

"I'm great!" Elaina jabbed her paintbrush into the air to emphasize her point.

"Why don't I take you home?" Sue said. "I made you a nice lunch."

"Peanut butter and mayo with sweet pickles on white bread?" Elaina asked, dropping her paint brush on the ground.

"With the bread buttered, just how you like it," Sue said, leading her grandmother away.

Monica turned her nose up in disgust. "She doesn't really eat that, does she?"

"The old folks who lived through the Depression have some crazy eats," Soapy said, "but you'd be surprised how good some of it is."

"Who died this time, Cameron Cripps-Hayman?" Roy Lancaster asked. I hadn't heard him come up behind me. Johnna Fitzgerald stood beside him, knitting bag slung over her walker. They were two of my volunteers helping to plan Canal Days. I had four seniors volunteering. Roy and Johnna seniors in age, and Anna Carmichael and Logan Foust seniors by grade. The four of us had been integral to solving the murder of the last victim I'd found.

"We're not sure yet," I said. "Mrs. Nelson found him," I added, quickly.

Between the numerous hours Roy clocked at the Cornerstone bar and the numerous hours Johnna spent gossiping with the women in town, the two of them would have a name before the police got the poor man's wallet out of his pocket.

"The poor dear," Johnna said. "I better start organizing a pot luck for after the funeral. Mourning always makes people hungry."

"Oh no," Monica said.

I followed her gaze down the road to the approaching car. "Mom."

"In all the excitement, I'd forgotten she was coming to see Dog Diggity today." Monica dropped her head into her hands. "She already thinks it's dumb of me to quit my job in Columbus and move here. Now *this* happens on the day she comes to visit."

"Welcome to the club," I said. For the past four years, ever since I moved to town, Mom thought it was a stupid move.

Ben's mother, Irene, had signed over Ellsworth House, the ancestral estate, to him when we got married. It was her way of luring him back to Metamora, and it worked. The town had grown on me, and I'd recently realized that I was right where I wanted to be. My mother would never understand that, though.

I slung an arm around Monica as Mom parked her Mercedes Benz beside Ben's truck. "We'll make her see reason," I said. "Don't worry."

"What's going on here?" Mom asked, striding over. She gave me air kisses and Monica a giant hug.

"Dead man behind the building," Roy blurted, rubbing his perpetually red nose.

"Cameron's a dead body magnet," Johnna added, helpfully.

Mom shot me a steely, narrowed-eyed look. "I told you nothing good would come from you moving here."

And so it began.

"Mom," I said, changing the subject, "let me introduce you to a few of our neighbors. Roy Lancaster and Johnna Fitzgerald are helping to organize Canal Days next weekend, and this is Soapy Thompson, our mayor."

I turned to Roy, Johnna, and Soapy. "This is Angela Cripps, my mother."

"And mine," Monica added.

"Of course." I stopped myself from rolling my eyes. A bad habit I'd picked up from my sixteen-year-old stepdaughter, Mia.

"Angela Cripps," Roy said, sauntering up beside Mom and eyeing her from the top of her sleek, dark brown bob cut to the toes of her impractical, beloved heels. "No modern-day hyphenated last name for you, then?" he asked.

Roy had a strong dislike for the practice of women keeping their maiden name and hyphenating with their husband's, which was the reason he always addressed me by my full name. To make a point.

"Legally," Mom said, eyeing him cooly, "my full name is Angela Zaborowski Cripps."

"Good Lord in heaven, woman! That's a mouthful." He shook his head, disapproving.

"Oh, you old duffer," Johnna said. "You're stuck in the fifties."

"Now that was a good decade." Roy smiled with nostalgia.

Ignoring them, I turned to Mom. "Why don't you go ahead to the house and get settled in? Mia should be there, and we'll be along soon."

Mom just wrapped her arm around Monica's shoulders and held tight. "I'm not leaving my daughters at a crime scene."

Monica closed her eyes and shivered.

I bit my tongue. I was the one who'd checked for the pulse of a dead man and I wasn't being half as dramatic as Monica.

"Why don't I treat you Cripps women to a hot drink?" Soapy said. "Our caramel apple latte is in season."

The Soapy Savant, in addition to selling homemade soaps and lotions, served a variety of coffees and teas.

"That would be lovely," Mom said. "Thank you so much."

"No rest for the weary," Roy said. "Come on, Johnna dear, let's get back to work. Some of us have Canal Days to put on."

"I'll be in to help!" I called after them as they shuffled along to the bridge that would take them to the other side of the canal, where our makeshift office was located two blocks back in the moldy basement of the old Metamora Friends and Family church.

With one week until Canal Days, I hoped news of the poor man behind our building wouldn't sink our hopes of drawing visitors to town.

∞

Soapy's caramel apple lattes could sooth the nerves of a cat on hot bricks. I took a sip and eased back in my chair, breathing in the spicy and floral scents of aromatic soaps and coffee.

"I don't know how you can be so calm," Mom said. "This will ruin your sister's business before she even gets the doors open."

The corners of my sister's mouth turned down and her lips quivered.

"Oh no," I said. "This town won't be detoured by a random act of violence that just happened to occur behind Dog Diggity."

"As someone who has worked in PR for most of her adult life," Mom said, sitting up straighter, "I'm telling you we need to spin this the right way so it doesn't impact your reputation."

I wasn't sure what was the right way to spin murder, but Monica perked up. "What should we do?" she asked.

"First, we need to get visible. We need to meet this head on. Acknowledge what happened and convey our deepest sympathies. We talk up the town."

Soapy's wife, Theresa, and I exchanged doubting glances. The people in this town could spot a ploy from ten miles away. If Mom went out exploiting a man's death for business profit, it would do more harm to Monica's business than the murder itself.

"I think we better wait until we have some facts," I said. "Right now we don't even know who the man is."

"It's never too soon to be proactive, Cameron," Mom said, waving me off.

"What are we being proactive about?" Ben asked, striding up to the table. "It better not be finding out who murdered Butch Landow." He pointed at me. "No meddling from you and your Metamora Clue Crew, or whatever you call yourselves."

"The Metamora Action Agency," I said, bristling. "And don't worry, we have enough going on planning Canal Days." The truth was, without my team of seniors, the last murder in this town would still be unsolved.

"Butch Landow?" Soapy said, handing Ben a cup of coffee. "He pretty much keeps to himself out there on that old farm. He's never been overly friendly, but I can't see why someone would want him dead."

"What was he doing behind my building?" Monica asked.

"I'm sorry," Ben said, "but I can't release any information about an ongoing case."

He didn't say he didn't know what Butch Landow was doing behind Dog Diggity, so that meant he must know something. All I had to do was find out what it was. After all, if I could solve a case with zero experience four months ago, I could only imagine how much better I'd be at it this time around. With Canal Days exactly one week from today, the quicker this case was put to bed, the better.

Ben rounded the table and kissed Mom on the cheek. "Good to see you, Angela."

Mom batted her thickly coated lashes and kissed his cheek in return, then wiped fuchsia lipstick from his cheek. The woman single-handedly kept Maybelline in business. She wouldn't even get the mail without having her "eyes on." One thing was for certain: Mom might've hated Metamora, but she adored Ben.

"I'm doing better knowing a strong, competent police officer is protecting my girls. How's my favorite son-in-law?" she cooed.

"Mia's living with us now," he said, then backtracked. "Well, she's living at the house with Cam. I don't have room for her at the Hilltop Castle gatehouse."

"Yes," Mom said, turning her gaze to me. "We'll have to see about that. You should be under the same roof as your daughter."

All eyes shifted to me, waiting for my response. It had been about ten months since Ben and I separated. There was nothing scandalous that went on, we simply grew apart. He worked nonstop and I was lost in a town I hadn't accepted and hadn't made my mark on. Neither of us wanted a divorce, but I had to be sure we wouldn't fall back into the same patterns if we started living together again.

Our romance had been a whirlwind, and we were married after two short months. Four years later, our relationship had stalled and we were giving it a much needed tune-up. By no means were either of us ready to trade it in for something new. We had a set movie night. We were having fun together again, and we were finding our way back.

I vowed that Angela Cripps would not sweep in and destroy the progress we'd made. Wasn't it enough to fend off my mother-in-law?

Now I had to deal with my own mom, too? This was suddenly looking like a good time to hop a plane and take a vacation across the ocean. On second thought, the moon might not even be far enough.

"What's the Hilltop Castle gatehouse?" Mom asked Ben when I ignored her comment. "I thought you were staying at a bed-and-breakfast in town."

"The man I work for, Carl Finch, he owns the castle that sits atop the hill out on Route 52," Ben explained. "I'm staying in his gatehouse. Kind of goes with the job, I guess."

Mom perked up. "He owns a castle?"

"A modern castle," Ben said. "He had it built."

"Ambitious. Is he single?" Mom's eyes narrowed as she shifted her gaze to Monica. I knew that shrewd look. She'd hunt down Carl Finch before the day was out. I liked Carl, but I didn't necessarily want him as my brother-in-law.

"It just so happens he is," Ben said and sauntered over beside me. He sat down and, attempting to be discreet, leaned in to whisper, "I need to tell you something."

"Okay."

"It's about—"

"Andy's being arrested!" my stepdaughter, Mia, shouted, bursting through the door and running to our table. "They're putting handcuffs on him and everything!"

"This is what you were going to tell me, wasn't it?" I asked Ben.

He nodded, tight lipped.

"What on earth could Sheriff Reins be thinking? Andy Beaumont is no murderer!" I shoved my chair back and flung my handbag over my shoulder. "If you'll all excuse me, I have a murder to solve."

"Cam," Ben said, grasping my wrist. "No."

"A Cripps woman doesn't know the word *no*." I cocked an eyebrow toward Mom and Monica. Both of them nodded and stood up with me.

Solidarity. It wasn't often found in my family, but when it happened, we were a threesome to be reckoned with.

· Two ·

Who's Andy?" Mom asked as the three of us walked across the bridge toward Ellsworth House. "Is he that handyman you told me about?"

"Yes, and he's a friend. There's no way he killed anybody."

Monica gave my shoulder a squeeze. "Don't worry. We'll find out who really did this. I already sent a text to Anna and Logan. They're going to start digging for information from the high school kids."

"The high school kids?" Mom asked. "What will teenagers know?"

"You'd be surprised," I said. "Mia's been at that school for a little under two months and she usually knows town gossip before I do."

Mom gave a little shrug. "Back when I was in high school us kids didn't concern ourselves with the goings on of our parents. We had much more interesting things in our own lives."

"More interesting than a murder in your town? The second in the same year?" My mother: the consummate contrarian.

Monica, paying no attention to us, nodded down the street. "Who's that? I've never seen him before."

13

In the distance, a man walked toward us with a dog on a leash. A big gray dog. Possibly bigger than Brutus, Ben's beast. "I don't know. Must be a tourist."

"Hmm ..." Monica stared at the man with interest. "Look how well he handles his dog. I wonder where he learned that."

"Somewhere they train dogs," I mused. "Something I need to invest in."

When we reached my house, Cassandra Platt was sitting on my front steps, crying and swatting away the bees that live in my porch columns. Cass and Andy started dating soon after he came to town.

"I'm so sorry," I told her, taking her hand and tugging her to her feet. "We'll get him out of this."

"Come inside," Monica said, opening the door. As soon as it was wide enough to let the dogs out, they charged through, slobbering and barking at their visitors.

"Get down!" Mom shouted, swatting Gus, the giant Newfoundland, with her handbag.

Cass, on the other hand, knelt down and had one arm around each of my twin mutts, scratching behind their erect, abnormally small ears. Wiry hair flew in the breeze, and their stout, tank-like bodies quivered in pleasure. "Did you name them yet?" she asked, smiling and snuffling back tears.

Dogs were always good for what ailed you.

"Not yet. Nothing seems quite right for them."

Mia's puppy, Liam, a tiny, white fur ball, came scampering to the door barking his shrill yip, trying to round up the canine troop of which he'd designated himself leader. The others ignored him, as usual.

"I *cannot* believe you have all of these wild animals in your home!" Mom said, brushing dog hair from her slacks.

I ushered the dogs and humans inside and down the hall to the kitchen, where I let the dogs out the back door and sat everyone else at the table. "Cass, why did they arrest Andy? What evidence could they possibly have?"

She took a deep breath and filled us in. "He called me this morning all shaken up. He stopped out at Landow Farm to ask Butch some questions about modern farming. He was filming when Butch opened the door. Butch had a fit and shoved Andy's camera in his face. It gave him a black eye! Andy said Butch ranted and raved about trespassers and his right to privacy on his own property, then he called the cops. Andy was gone before they got there, but that's why Reins questioned him to begin with. He'd been out to the farm this morning, and when he saw Andy's black eye, he assumed Andy and Butch were fighting just before Butch was found dead."

"That would be the most obvious situation to have happened," Mom said.

"But it didn't," Monica was quick to interject. "Andy would never do that."

"Oh, I didn't mean to imply ..." Mom trailed off, clutching her necklace.

"Of course he didn't do anything." I rounded the counter and opened the pantry. This day called for some of Betty Platt's cookie's from Grandma's Cookie Cutter, the bakery two doors down that I found impossible to stay out of. I piled fat molasses cookies onto a plate with some chewy chocolate chip and set them in the center of the table. "Nobody saw Butch after that, Cass?"

She shook her head. "I guess not. He lives alone, and all of his farm hands were out in the fields working."

This situation was bad. The black eye and trespassing call gave Andy motive in the eyes of the law. "Andy was here alone when Butch was shot, wasn't he?" I asked, knowing Mia would have been working at the Soda Pop shop until lunch, when she'd come home to find him being hauled away.

"Yes," Cass said, breaking a cookie into pieces and dropping them on a napkin. "He has no alibi."

I felt like that cookie looked. How in the world would we get Andy out of jail when the police believed he had the motive and the opportunity? We would have to find another suspect. Someone wanted Butch Landow dead, and all I had to do was figure out who.

"What do you know about Butch, Cass?" I'd never met the man myself. He kept to himself, and was known to be reclusive.

"Not too much. His ex-wife, Phillis, is Fiona Stein's cousin. Fiona's husband, Jim, is—was—good friends with Butch, I think."

Monica tapped her fingernails on the table. "So it stands to reason that if Jim Stein was friends with Butch, then his cronies—Stew Hayman and Jefferson Briggs—would be friends with him, too."

"I've never heard Stew mention him," I said, referring to my father-in-law. "Not that he and I have a lot of conversations about who he pals around with."

"What about this Phillis?" Mom asked. "It's always the ex."

Cass shrugged. "I've only met her a couple of times. She and Butch were still married then. I think they've only been divorced for a couple of years."

"We need to find out about her. Fiona is our best contact for that," Monica said, catching my eye.

"Don't look at me," I said. "That woman has no love for me. She harasses me every month to pay my fines to the Daughters of Historical Metamora for the unapproved colors I painted my house."

Cass let out a small chuckle. "At our last meeting, they were talking about how much money we were short and how we wouldn't be able to fund our annual matching sweatshirts to wear to Canal Days. Your mother-in-law was hot under the collar about you not paying your fines." Cass grinned, wiping the last stray tear from her cheek. "I say good riddance to those ugly sweatshirts."

"Don't let Irene hear you say that." I couldn't help the surge of glee that spread through me at the thought of ruining my mother-in-law's plans. She and her Daughters of Metamora gang ruled the town with an iron fist. Or tried to. I wouldn't be bullied by any of them.

Monica drummed her fingers on the table again, eyeing me. "Well … maybe if you took Fiona a check for their sweatshirts she'd be willing to have a chat about her cousin."

"Where, exactly, am I going to get a check that doesn't turn to rubber the minute I touch it with ink? I don't have the money to pay Irene's fine even if I wanted to. Which I don't, I might add."

"Cameron Corrine Cripps," Mom said. When she pulled out the triple C's, I knew I was in for it. "If I've told you once, I've told you a million times. You win more flies with honey than you do with vinegar."

"I bet you have a lot of honey in your porch columns," Cass said.

I snorted. "That's about the only thing keeping this house together."

"I'm serious!" Mom whacked her palm on the table. "Pretend to like this woman even if you can't stand the sight of her. I'll give you the money to pay the fine, and I'll butter up Irene. Monica can work on that Carl Finch fellow."

Monica leaned forward a bit. "What does Carl Finch have to do with this?"

"Nothing," Mom said. "But he's rich and single, isn't he? I swear, I don't know how you girls survive for one day without me."

"It's a mystery," I muttered, shoving a bite of cookie past my lips before I said something I'd end up regretting.

Across the table, Cass focused over my shoulder. "That's Andy's video camera."

I turned around to find it sitting on my countertop beside the toaster. "Wouldn't they want that for evidence?"

"In this clown cop town?" Mom said, smirking. "It's a miracle they even thought to question Andy, let alone come up with a motive. You can't expect them to take evidence too, can you?"

"Sheriff Reins is a good police officer," I said, thinking it sounded a bit over-reaching out loud. Reins was a qualified, dedicated officer. Whether he was a good one was up to interpretation and circumstance.

Cass got up and hustled over to where Andy's camera sat. "It still has the tape in it. Let's watch it and see if there's anything that proves he's innocent."

I followed her into the living room. "I hope you know how to hook it up to the TV."

"I've watched him do it a hundred times at least."

Mom and Monica came in and took a seat on the couch. I sat on the floor beside Cass and turned the TV to video input while she hooked up one end of a cord that looked like my phone charger to a slot in the back and the other to the camera.

The screen went blue, then popped on with an image of a gravel driveway leading up to a ramshackle old farm house.

"Here we go," Cass said.

The picture was shaky as Andy walked up to the door of the white house. His arm came into view as he reached forward and knocked.

"Why would he want to record this?" Mom asked. "Who cares about a guy answering his front door?"

"It brings the viewer into the moment," Cass answered. She'd obviously learned a lot about filming documentaries over the past almost-year that she and Andy had been together.

Andy knocked again, and the door opened. A lean, grizzled older man stood in the doorway. I didn't recognize him as the man on the bench, but I'd only seen him lying on his stomach, so this was the first I'd ever seen his face. His skin was leathery, and thin lips tightened into an angry line.

"Get that camera out of here! Who sent you? Arnie Rutherford? I've had enough of you trespassers on my property! Leave! Now!" Butch's hand came up fast toward the camera and the picture went black.

"Hey!" Andy shouted, and the sound of scuffling came through my speakers. The picture came to life again with the green needles on a box bush whizzing by in an arc, then a cracking noise as the camera hit the ground, then all we could see was a sidewalk, sideways on the television, Butch retreating back inside, and the door slamming shut.

"Gah! My eye," Andy said to himself, and the camera was righted. He must've grabbed it. Then the screen went black.

"That must be it," I said, looking at Cass. But the words were out of my mouth no more than a second when the video came back on.

"Please don't be busted," Andy said, gazing into the eye of the camera. He gently brushed the edge of the lens. Then the video went black once more.

"Wait!" Monica hopped up off the couch. "Rewind that part. Is there a slow motion?"

"Probably," Cass said. "Let me see."

She rewound the footage and pressed play. Andy's face appeared again.

"Right there!" Monica yelled, darting toward the TV. Her finger touched the screen behind Andy's shoulder. "See them? In the distance. I think those are two men."

I leaned forward, closer to the TV and squinted. I really needed to get to an optometrist. "Maybe..."

"Beside the trees?" Cass asked. "Yeah, I think I see two men."

19

Mom came up behind me and leaned in over my head with a hand on my shoulder to get a better look. "One is a little taller than the other. It's hard to make out any features when they're against those trees."

"Can you zoom in?" Monica asked.

"I wish I knew how to work this thing." Cass pressed buttons on the camera and my television and managed to fast forward, change the screen aspect to letter box, and bring up closed captioning in Spanish. "Ugh. I need directions. They can't keep Andy forever, right? I mean, I'll be able to talk to him soon, won't I?"

"Of course," I said, patting her leg. "We'll tell him about this and we'll find out who those two men are."

"Don't forget Arnie Rutherford," Mom said. "He's the first person who sprung to our murder victim's mind when he saw Andy."

"Whoever he is, he shouldn't be too hard to find," I said, getting up, and finding that with each passing year the floor was farther and farther away from a standing position—or at least harder to lift my weight off of.

I retrieved my laptop from the dining room table and sat between Mom and Monica on the couch. Cass went around to the back where she could lean over and watch as I typed *Arnie Rutherford* into the search engine.

"Attorney at law," I read, clicking on the website link. "A real estate attorney."

"Why would Butch think Andy was a real estate attorney?" Cass wondered out loud behind me.

"Well, that's an easy one," Mom said. She shifted her gaze from each of us in turn, then shook her head. "Hello, girls! His ex probably wants the farm!"

I quickly came to the next logical question. "So if she couldn't get it from him, who gets it now that he's dead?"

"I think you better pay Fiona Stein a visit," Monica said. "Sorry, Cass, looks like you'll have to wear an ugly sweatshirt to Canal Days after all."

"If it proves Andy's innocence, I'll wear one every day for the rest of my life."

"Young love," Mom said, and reached over and squeezed Monica's hand.

"Carl Finch isn't young, Mom," she said.

A cacophony of barking started up in the backyard. I hopped up, thankful for the distraction before Mom tried to tangle me in her matchmaking web. "Gotta let the dogs in. Duck and cover."

The sound of Mom and Monica bickering was quickly overtaken by hearty barks and Liam's shrill yip. Never in the four months since adopting my furry friends had I been thankful for the holy ruckus they made. Until now. How could I have forgotten what living with my mother and sister under the same roof was like?

And we'd be adding Mia to the mix. How in the world would I survive the week?

Good gravy, I was in for it.

· Three ·

In all the pandemonium of the afternoon, I'd almost forgotten John Bridgemaker and Paul Foxtracker's BBQ that night at the Metamora Mound Builders' Association lodge. John was the president of the MMBA, and Paul was the town's representative at the national level for the Native American Council.

The lodge was packed from wall to wall. Hank Jenkins from the BBQ Shack set up in the parking lot and the aroma had my mouth watering. Carl Finch provided the side dishes, set up in a buffet beside a cash bar that ran along the back wall of the lodge. Friends and neighbors milled around long tables set up in rows with plastic cups of beer and wine.

"Welcome, Cam." John gave me a big hug.

"I almost didn't recognize you, John," I said. He'd traded his usual jeans and leather vest for a pair of tan slacks and white oxford shirt.

"*I* almost didn't recognize me," he joked. "Thanks for coming, Monica." He hugged my sister and then took Mom by the hand. "You must be the youngest Cripps sister."

Mom batted her eyes demurely. "Aren't you a charmer?"

"John Bridgemaker," I said, "this is my mother—and Monica's, of course—Angela Cripps."

"Honored to make your acquaintance," John said, and I could swear my mother blushed. He was definitely a good-looking man, but not one I would ever peg for someone who could flush Angela Cripps's cheeks.

"If I can have your attention, please," Paul Foxtracker spoke into a microphone from the front of the room. Everyone fell silent and turned their attention in his direction. "Thank you all for coming tonight. I hope you're enjoying the food and friends. While we have you all gathered here together, the Metamora Mound Builders' Association has some exciting news to announce. We're looking into building a casino right here in town. It'll generate tourism and bring jobs. The initial stages of this operation require a majority approval by our residents. Now I know you all will have a lot of questions. We welcome all of you to our planning meetings to get answers and engage in discussions. In the meantime, eat, drink, and enjoy!"

Slowly, the chit-chat in the room reengaged. "A casino?" I asked John, stupefied by the announcement. Our quaint little town the site of a casino? I couldn't wrap my head around it.

"Yes," he said, grinning from ear to ear. "We've studied the numbers, weighed the benefits, and we're confident a casino is the right business venture and this is the right time to do it."

"Well ..." Tongue tied, I couldn't get my questions in line. They all wanted to rush out at the same time. "Not downtown by the canal, surely?"

"No, no. We need a lot of land to build. We're looking at a few properties." He leaned in and whispered in my ear. "Maybe it's too soon, but I don't believe you knew Butch Landow, did you?"

"No. Today was the first I'd ever ... uh ... come across him."

"We were looking into buying his farm. He owed—well, let's just say, we were making him an offer he couldn't refuse for too much longer. Unfortunately, today's tragedy has complicated things somewhat."

"You wanted to buy—wait." My head spun. Arnie Rutherford, the real estate attorney—was he representing John and the association, and not Phillis? "You talked to him about buying his farm and he said no?"

"Not that it matters now. What a terrible way to go. I can't say I'm surprised, though. From what I understand, he made a few enemies over the years."

"Really?"

"Hey, John. Nice spread." Ben came up beside me and shook John's hand. Mom and Monica had walked off at some point while John and I were speaking. I looked around and found them at the bar with my in-laws, Irene and Stewart, and Mia, who still wore her Soda Pop Shop uniform: a bright pink shirt with a red-and-white striped apron. She turned around and I saw she had a tray laden with fudge. Sue Nelson was in charge of dessert at this shindig. She made the best fudge around.

"I was just telling Cameron about the casino," John said, refocusing my attention.

"That's right," I said. "He was telling me where they were hoping to build." I gave Ben a tap in the back of his leg to let him know something was up.

"What?" Ben asked, turning to me.

"What, what?"

"Why did you hit me in the leg?"

Oh good gravy. "Accident. Sorry." You would think after almost five years of marriage, Ben would know me a little bit better by now.

"I'm going to go say hello to your parents. John, I'm looking forward to hearing more about the casino."

I hustled off before the urge to knock some sense into Ben got too strong to resist and I whacked him with my handbag. Too bad I'd downsized. I'd fill him in later on John's attempt to buy the Landow farm. In the meantime, I needed to work on spreading honey with the Daughters. Too bad I've always found honey hard to spread.

On my way across the room to the bar, I said a quick prayer that something miraculous might happen to stop me from having to make nice with my mother-in-law. The first thing out of her mouth would be about my delinquent fine, or her taking something else from my house.

My stomach dropped as I caught sight of my mom hugging Irene, the two laughing like old school pals. I knew Mom was doing it for my benefit, but seeing them all chummy made me wary. The last thing I wanted was a total turn around from Irene and finding myself being inducted into her petty little club as a Hayman ancestor by marriage. I wanted Irene softened up, not all gooey.

Their gazes landed on me, and both reached out at the same time, still laughing. "Come talk to us," Mom said, her eyes a little glittery from the wine. "You've been so serious since I got here. Let's relax and enjoy our visit."

Did she forget she showed up when a dead man was found behind Dog Diggity?

She shot me a sly wink, letting me know she was putting on this happy act for Irene.

"It's good to see you, dear," Irene said, taking my hand and pulling me in for an air kiss. "Stewart, order Cameron a glass of wine."

My father-in-law gave me a quick smile and turned to the bartender.

"I hear Canal Days is coming along nicely," Irene said, beaming at me. Mom had clearly put her under some sort of spell.

"It is," I said. "All of our shops are participating and getting ready. We even have a few vendors from Brookville and Connersville setting up tables."

"None of the vendors who sell those home party type of products, I hope," she said. "If I wanted wax candle melts, I'd buy the handmade version from Ike's. They're much better quality. Everything made here in town is."

Ike's Candle Company was one of the oldest shops in Metamora. He took it over from his father, who took it over from his, and so on. Unfortunately for Irene, Ike was the last male in his line and there were no females left in the Daughters, either. It was rather sad to think about the town's family tree losing a limb.

"Only our small independent businesses and crafters have tables," I said, easing her mind, although I happened to buy my handbag from one of those parties. Cass hosted it at her inn for a friend of hers.

Stewart handed me a glass of white wine. I took a sip, knowing if I finished even one glass I'd have a headache. Red wine was the way to go if you wanted to avoid headaches. Unfortunately, my taste buds abhorred most red wine.

Mom pulled Monica into our little huddle. "Guess who's giving the Daughter's of Metamora free samples for their dogs?" Mom trilled.

"Who better to get feedback from than the women in town?" Monica said, her smile twitching at the corners.

Mom's helping hand might just stick Monica and I permanently under Irene's thumb. "That's great. Very nice of you," I said.

"If only you planned to sell cat goodies," Irene said. "Most of us are cat people, you know. We like a more dignified animal in our homes."

"Right," Monica said, nodding, her stiff smile fading a bit. "I'll keep that in mind."

I had nothing against cats. I let one in my house on a regular basis. Although I couldn't keep him out if I wanted to, and I wasn't sure Spook actually qualified as a normal cat. But dogs could be dignified, too. Not *my* dogs, but someone's dogs, I was sure. Like that man we'd seen walking his down the street earlier today. That was a dignified dog. At least from a distance.

"And speaking of generous," Irene said. "Your darling mother has offered to pay the fine for your house. It still needs repainted, mind you, but your debt will be up-to-date."

"Right," I said. Then figured I'd better look like this was news to me. "Great! Thanks, Mom." I leaned in to give Mom a hug, but was stopped by the bewildered expression on her face as she looked over my shoulder out into the room.

"What's going on?" She asked.

Then a woman started screaming.

I turned to see the commotion in the front of the room travel to the center, following the wake of an older woman with short silver hair wearing a long, flowing black dress. "John Bridgemaker killed my husband!" she shouted.

"Oh no," Irene said. "That's Phillis Landow."

Fiona Stein rushed up to her cousin's side and took her arm, trying to calm her. Phillis shook her off. "I will *not* be silenced! That man"—she pointed to John—"*murdered* Butch!"

Ben hustled up to her, raising his hands like he was warding off any more outbursts. "Mrs. Landow, let's go outside and I'll take your statement."

"I just gave you my statement! John Bridgemaker shot Butch in the back! Write that down!"

"I'll need more than that if you want to make it official."

Phillis lifted her chin and took a deep breath, puffing out her chest. "Fine. I'll make an official statement, and that man"—she pointed to John again—"better end up behind bars for life!"

Ben took her arm and hooked it through his, escorting her back to the front of the room and out the doors.

"What a scene!" Mom said, shaking her head. "I wouldn't have believed it if I hadn't seen it with my own eyes."

"I thought they were divorced?" I asked Irene.

"They are. Have been for three years. She's never accepted it, poor thing."

Mia, totally unfazed, stuck her tray out between us. "Fudge?"

I wanted to be annoyed by her lack of sensitivity, but really, who didn't want fudge at a time like this? "Thanks," I said, taking a piece of chocolate with walnuts.

"Stress eating," Mia said, shaking her head. "Gets you every time."

She walked away before I could threaten to ground her.

"She's right," Irene said, wagging her finger. "Women who have weight problems often eat when they're stressed."

Monica found my hand and squeezed it, silently reminding me that we didn't need another dead person in town. Today was not the day to strangle my mother-in-law.

Then Cass rushed up to me, frazzled. Another suspect could take the focus off of Andy. Maybe the outburst was good news after all.

"Have you heard anything?" I asked, trying to angle my body to block out Irene. The last thing I needed was for her to eavesdrop on our conversation.

"He just called, finally," she said, cradling her cell phone in both hands. "They aren't releasing him until bond can be set on Monday."

"Monday? You're kidding me. That's crazy."

"He told me how to zoom in on the tape, Cam. We have to find out who was in the tree line this morning at Landow's when Andy was filming."

I looked around. Phillis's display had effectively killed the party. "Well, this BBQ is dead. Let's go."

"We're leaving?" Mom said, looking stricken. "But we haven't even eaten yet, and I've been having such a nice time catching up with your in-laws."

"Stay," Irene said. "Unless Ben comes back, we'll be dropping Mia off, so it's no problem taking you along as well."

"What a lovely idea," Mom said. "It's so rare to have another like-minded woman to chat with."

"I'm coming with you," Monica said to me, recoiling.

"Good, because you drove."

Irene stepped forward and took me by both arms. "I'll stop by this week and visit. I want to make sure those dogs aren't tearing up Ellsworth house."

My mind flashed to the bottom of the newel post that had been gnawed by Liam. His tiny teeth were razor sharp. I'd have to get Andy to—oh good gravy. Andy couldn't fix anything from jail.

Time to find a new handyman, and fast!

· Four ·

"Holy cow, is that really him?" I couldn't believe my eyes. Like earlier, Cass and I sat on the floor in front of the TV. Monica sat on her knees behind us, peering over our heads.

"Who's that with him?" Monica asked. "Is that the guy who spoke tonight?"

"Yes, that's Paul Foxtracker." Cass shook her head in disbelief. "Phillis was right. It was John."

I couldn't deny that seeing John Bridgemaker and his friend, Paul, lurking in the trees on Butch's property—the property they wanted to purchase to build their casino—on the morning of the day he died … well, that was definitely suspicious.

I couldn't wrap my mind around John killing anyone, though. He was all about nature and peace and promoting education and appreciation for his culture. Killing Butch didn't exactly factor into that plan.

Monica was oddly silent. Her brow was furrowed like her mind was churning through all of the facts and couldn't believe what her eyes were showing her.

Cass twisted her fingers together. "They have to let Andy out, right? I mean, I have to take this to Reins and Ben. This is enough proof to arrest John and Paul."

"Right." I clicked off the TV. "You better get it over to them so Andy can come home."

Cass unhooked the camera from the TV. "Thanks for being here for me, and for Andy. I don't know what either of us would do without you." She gave me a big hug, sighing in relief.

"Go get him," I said, urging her to her feet. "Wait. First help me up."

She and Monica tugged me off the floor, and Cass gave us a quick wave as she ran to the front door.

"Something's not right," Monica said as soon as the door shut behind Cass.

"I know. I was hoping it was just me, but even with the evidence and Phillis's accusation, I can't imagine John taking Butch's life."

"Honestly, I don't think even Cass was convinced. The proof is clear, though. What were they doing on Butch's property? Did he know they were there?"

"The way they were lurking in the trees, I doubt it."

Monica followed me into the kitchen. I tugged the refrigerator door open, hoping food had magically restocked on the shelves. "We have cheese, strawberry jelly, and outdated milk."

"The cheese is for the dog treats," Monica said with a severe look of warning.

"I won't touch your cheese. Promise."

"I used all the peanut butter last week." She stood on her toes and peered over my shoulder. "We need to go to the store."

"Well, what else do I have to do on a Saturday night?" I closed the fridge and grabbed my handbag off the counter.

"You can help me make more treats when we get home. I need to buy flour. Cass gave me some of her fresh picked basil yesterday, and

I'm adding it to my Diggity Cheese Snaps recipe. Basil's a natural anti-inflammatory, so it should help Isobel's arthritis." Monica jingled her car keys and knelt down to pet Isobel, who was snoozing beside the fridge.

I opened the back door and yelled for my canine herd. "Get in here. I can't let you stay outside barking or Irene will fine me for being a menace to the town."

Once Gus, the twin tanks, and little Liam bounded inside, Monica and I ambled out to the car. "How long do you think they'll have Dog Diggity taped off?" she asked as we drove. "I need to get back in there or we won't be ready to open by next weekend."

"I don't know. We can ask Ben."

Out on 52, heading toward Brookville, the MMBA lodge came into view. Blue and white flashing lights filled the parking lot. I lunged forward, grasping the dashboard. "They're arresting John! Pull in!"

Monica turned the wheel and parked on the side of the building. The BBQ guests were filing out of the building, shaking their heads in disbelief. Some got in their cars and drove away while others stood in groups gawking and gossiping. I spotted Mom and Irene craning their necks for a better look, standing with Mia and Stewart, Fiona Stein and her husband Jim, Elaina Nelson, Carl Finch, and Steve Longo, owner of Odd and Strange Metamora.

We hustled toward them as two of Brockville's finest escorted John and Paul out of the lodge in handcuffs. I spotted Ben beside the front door, keeping our friends and neighbors at bay while the police did their jobs.

I ran up to him. "What's going on?" It was a stupid question. I knew what was going on. Cass turned in the video, but could it really have happend this fast? But what else was there to say when I was still in disbelief that it was actually happening? "Are they releasing Andy?"

Ben took me by the arm and ushered me aside. "I know you're invested in this case, being that it's Andy, but I need you to stand aside and stay out of this."

I crossed my arms over my chest like a petulant child. "I was the one who helped Cass find the video, or these arrests wouldn't even be happening right now!"

As soon as I said it, I wanted to suck the words right back into my mouth.

Ben gave me The Sigh and The Look. His patented *Ben is exasperated, leave him alone* look, accompanied by a rattling sigh from his depths that sounded like he couldn't put up with me for one more second. The look that made me wonder how I could be so stupid, even if I didn't think I'd been stupid at all. The sigh that inflicted guilt, even if I didn't know what I felt guilty about. He had The Sigh and The Look down to a science.

"Go home, Cam," he said, and turned and walked back to the door.

Deflated but simmering with annoyance and curiosity, I made my way over to where Monica and Mom were standing with Irene and her huddle. "Ben wouldn't tell me anything," I announced before they pounced.

"They have this all wrong," Stewart said, shaking his head. "John and Paul are the last people they should be fingering for Butch's murder."

It sounded like he had a hunch who the police *should* be suspecting. "They must have enough evidence to arrest them," I said, hoping to prod his thoughts on the matter.

"Can't be anything substantial. Those two didn't have any business with him. No reason to want him dead."

"Hmm…" I sidestepped closer to my father-in-law. "I heard they wanted to buy Landow Farm, but Butch wouldn't sell."

"Well, he sure and shoot ain't selling now, is he? They have nothing to gain from Butch being dead. Now that farm goes into probate and will be tied up forever with Phillis trying to get her grubby paws on it."

Fiona shot a nasty look back at us over her shoulder. Stewart held up a hand and gave her an apologetic smile. She snapped her head back around.

"You think Phillis had a part in his death?" I whispered.

"I don't know. Love and hate, you know what they say, there's a fine line."

"She didn't seem very stable tonight either," I said.

"Phillis has always been one apple shy of a bushel."

"Sounds like the perfect suspect."

Stewart nodded. "Only problem is she was in Cincinnati at some art exhibit from last night until late this afternoon when she got back and breezed in here like the Wicked Witch of the West."

"Art exhibit?"

"She's an artist. Some kind of sculptures. Makes no sense to me. The woman has to live off of donations or sponsors funding her while she creates her masterpieces."

To me it sounded like she could benefit from selling that farm and raking in all the cash. Would it motivate her to murder her ex-husband?

The police cars sped off, leaving the pockets of people in the parking lot with nothing to stare at. My stomach grumbled, reminding me that I hadn't fed it. Hank Jenkins was putting away all of his BBQ supplies. "I wonder if Hank has any left overs," I said, nudging Monica. "I'm starving."

"Stress eating," Irene said, with a *tsk tsk*.

"We haven't eaten dinner yet! I'm not stressed! I'm truly starving!"

Mom's eyes grew wide. "See if he has some *honey* for those biscuits, Cam," she said.

"Right. Honey." I gritted my teeth and stalked across the lot toward Hank with Monica on my heels.

"Hi, Cameron," Hank said, holding up a pair of tongs in greeting. "Come for the food and stay for the show, huh?"

"Actually, I didn't manage to get any food earlier. You wouldn't happen to have anything left?"

"It's your lucky day. I have chicken and ribs and some pulled pork sandwiches."

My mouth watered. "Give me two of everything."

"I hope some of that's for me," Monica said.

"I don't share my BBQ."

"I'll throw in extra," Hank said, laughing.

"What do you think about all of this?" I asked, waving a hand out behind me. "Crazy, isn't it?"

"I don't know, Cam. Sometimes I think the whole world has gone insane and this place was the last spot left on Earth. I guess it had to reach us some time."

"But Andy being arrested, and now John and Paul. I can't see any of them hurting someone."

"No, I can't either, but then again, it's usually someone the victim knows. At least that's what I learned from watching true crime shows on TV."

"I guess that's true."

"Nobody likes to think that one of their neighbors could do something like that, but every criminal has neighbors."

I pondered this as he stacked our foam boxes filled with BBQ. Every man and woman in jail had neighbors and friends, family and coworkers. How many of those people were shocked when they found out the person who lived next door was in jail for murder? Why did I think I was exempt from having someone in our tiny town commit such a terrible crime?

"Here you go," Hank said, passing a bulging plastic bag over his grill. "I threw in some baked beans and coleslaw."

"Sounds heavenly," Monica said. "Smells heavenly, too."

"Thanks, Hank," I said, holding the bag close. If this day brought one good thing, it would be this BBQ, and nothing was going to happen to it before I got it home.

On our way back to the car, my cell phone rang. I passed the food to Monica and answered.

"They're not releasing Andy," Cass said, sobbing into the phone. "They're keeping all three of them."

"What? Are they going to arrest the whole town until they can figure out who did it? They can't do that! Can they?"

"They say he could've been there with John and Paul. He might have created a diversion while the other two did—I don't know what! Something! They think they acted together since all three were on the film and at the farm at the same time."

"Oh, good gravy. Don't worry, Cass. I'll get to the bottom of this."

Right after I ate my BBQ.

∞

Stomach full and fingers sticky, I leaned back in my chair at the kitchen table. Across from me, Monica's eyes were hazy. "That was the best BBQ I've ever eaten," she said. "Now I'm going to go sleep for a week."

"So much for making dog treats."

"We didn't get to the store. I'll have to go tomorrow." She looked down at Isobel, who lay at her feet. "She's happy with the bites of chicken I gave her, anyway."

I'd tried to give my rib bones to the dogs and Monica almost had a conniption fit. Little did I know that any kind of cooked bone could splinter and get caught in the dog's throat. I just knew dogs loved bones. Monica had really been studying up and knew her stuff.

"I don't know what I'm going to do without Andy helping me get Dog Diggity ready. He was building shelves and some display tables and new shutters for the windows."

"We'll find someone to help. This town is full of handy people who know how to do things like that."

I really didn't know who we could ask, though. Everyone with a store was busy getting their own displays ready for Canal Days. Stewart might help out, but that would give Irene an opening to get her paws and influence in Dog Diggity. He'd have to be our last resort.

The front door opened and Mia came stomping inside. She slammed the door, tossed her apron on the floor and yelled, "My dad is such a jerk!"

"Whoa," I said, standing up. "Calm down and tell us what happened."

"I tried to ask him if I could go out with this guy, and he totally freaked. He said I was too young to date. I'm sixteen! When I tried to argue, he said he was too busy to deal with me and sent me home with Grandpa Stewart."

"Who's the guy?" Monica asked.

"Nobody now! I'm not allowed to go out with him, so what does it matter?"

"I'll talk to him, okay?" I had no idea what good that would do. He sent me home tonight, too. We were both on his naughty list, apparently.

Liam skittered around Mia's legs, jumping and yipping. She scooped him up and nuzzled him. "I'm going to bed. I have to work tomorrow."

I knew that meant she was going to lay in bed talking on her phone to Steph all night, complaining about how unfair her dad was being— a conversation that would surely dominate their workday tomorrow as well.

Mia stomped up the stairs, leaving Monica and I wondering where our mom had gotten off to. "Weren't Irene and Stewart supposed to drop her off?" Monica asked.

"I'll call her."

I dialed her number and it rang and rang. "She's not answering." A gnawing feeling erupted in my stomach. Or it was heartburn from the BBQ. "Where could she be?" I left a voicemail asking her to call me and hung up.

"Maybe her ringer is turned off," Monica said, clearing the table. "She does that a lot."

"You're not worried?"

Monica had lived with Mom, and then near her after she moved out, for a lot longer than I had. Plus, the two of them worked together and Monica was always the favorite.

Monica shrugged. "She's a grown woman. She doesn't need a babysitter."

"That's a strange thing to say."

"Why? What's so strange about it?

"What if something happened to her?"

"What could happen to her at a BBQ with your in-laws?"

"I don't know, but she's not here and she's not answering her phone."

Monica rubbed her forehead. "Trust me. She's fine."

"What's going on? There's something you're not telling me."

She turned away, stuffing the foam boxes into the trash. "Nothing's going on, Cam."

"That doesn't sound convincing."

"It's not my place to tell you, okay?"

The gnawing sensation grew. It definitely wasn't heartburn. "To tell me what?"

She leaned over the counter, resting on her elbows and propping her head in her hands. "Mom and Dad. They're divorced. They've been apart for a little over a year."

"What? *Divorced?* Nobody told me!"

"You had your own marriage to worry about, Cam. Mom didn't want you to worry about them. Their marriage was over a long time ago. They were basically roommates. One day they decided to talk about it and discovered they both wanted to see other people, so they got divorced."

"Just like that?"

"Just like that." She turned and opened the cupboard. "I'll make some coffee."

"Coffee? That's going to make this right?"

"There's nothing wrong about this, Cam. It's just new to you. They're both happier than they have been in years."

"What about that birthday present you brought me a few months ago? It was from both of them."

"Mom knows Dad is terrible with remembering dates. She put his name on it like she always has."

"I can't believe this." I sat down hard in my chair, head reeling.

"She was planning on telling you tonight, but after showing up to a dead man behind the store, she figured it could wait a little longer."

"Well, why not? I mean, it's already been a *year.*"

"Don't be upset, Cam. We didn't want you dealing with this and Ben. You weren't there, so you didn't need to know."

"I didn't need to know my parents are divorced? What about holidays? They were both there last Christmas."

"They've been together for the majority of their lives. They both wanted the divorce, but they're still friends and even go to dinner sometimes. Spending the holidays together with their kids isn't so strange."

"I feel so duped."

Monica sat a mug of hot coffee in front of me. "Well, don't worry. Mom's just fine. So is Dad."

"I just wish she would answer her phone."

Monica let out a groan. "I didn't want to say this, but I know where she is. She told me when you were talking to Ben, when John and Paul were being arrested."

"Where is she?"

"Getting a tour of Carl Finch's castle."

Oh good gravy. Carl Finch wasn't going to end up being my brother-in-law, he was going to end up being my stepdad!

· Five ·

All of this honey was drowning me, and not in niceties. There were more buzzing pests showing up at my house each day. My porch columns looked about ready to burst.

"You need a hive," a voice said from behind me.

I turned on my step ladder, where I was busy spraying bug repellant, and almost fell off. Old Dan stood on my sidewalk, looking up at me, while Elaina Nelson, in her Sunday best—shiny hot pink patent leather shoes and purse plus a black-and-white polka dot dress— hopped up the cement steps to stand next to me. Shading her eyes with her white gloved hand, she started singing. "*One hundred fu-zzy bees on the porch, one hundred fu-zzy bees. Take one down, swat him around, ninety-nine fu-zzy bees on the porch.*"

"I need to get *rid* of a hive," I clarified for Old Dan. Maybe he was having one of his senior moments.

"No, you need to get those honey bees out of there and into a hive." He worked the chaw tucked behind his lip and spit on the ground. "I'll build you one—have them out of there in no time."

"You can do that?" I shouted over Elaina's obnoxious crooning.

"You let me have some of the honey, and consider it done."

"It's a deal." I jogged down the porch steps and shook his hand.

Elaina's singing tapered off, and she ambled down to stairs to join us. "I was just trying to convince this old man to take me to dinner," she said. "We make a nice pair, don't we, Cameron? Old Dan and Grandma Diggity."

"Grandma Diggity?" I chuckled.

"Grandma Diggity is hip," she said, wiggling her hips, attempting some hip-hop dance move.

"Speaking of hips, don't break one." I hooked an arm through hers before she fell over in my yard.

"Shake it don't break it!" she shouted, then burst out laughing.

Old Dan spit on the ground, unfazed by her attempts to lure him into buying her dinner.

"Why don't you both come inside? I was just about to give up on those bees and go in and get Sunday dinner cooking. I'd love it if you both could stay and eat."

"What are we having?" Elaina asked, skipping to the porch.

"Lasagna. Monica went grocery shopping for most of the ingredients, but I'll get the sauce on so it's ready to put together."

I had a couple glass canning jars of tomatoes Cass had put up over the summer. They'd make a nice sauce.

I opened the door and invited the town's two oldest residents inside, standing with my legs spread and my arms outstretched to hold off the canine stampede. "Stay down!" I commanded as Gus stood on his back legs and rested his paws on my shoulders. In answer, he gave me a big, wet lick on the cheek. Liam skittered between my feet, jumping on Elaina's shins.

"Watch my stockings, you little runt!" she said, swiping him up off the floor into her arms. "Aren't you just the feistiest little cat ever!"

"He's no cat," Dan said.

Elaina held Liam out, examining him. "Looks like a Persian I used to own. Best cat I ever had. Wonder what ever happened to him?"

"You still have him," Dan said. "Why'd ya think your screened-in porch is covered in white fuzz?"

"I thought that was from the cottonwood trees."

If I didn't know that Sue made a daily visit to Elaina's house to make sure the cat was fed, the oven was turned off, and the bathroom wasn't flooded, I'd be concerned for the poor cat. Plus, I'd seen Elaina's cat outside a few times, carousing with Spook, the sneaky black cat who sometimes showed up in my house through a yet-to-be-found attic entrance.

"Looks like your hounds have been using your woodwork for a chew toy," Old Dan said, toeing the bottom of my newel post.

"I know, and Irene's going to have a fit when she sees it. I was hoping Andy could fix it for me, but now that he's in jail and we don't know when he's getting out…"

"I'll fix it for ya. Just need an hour or two and it's as good as new."

"Really? I didn't know you were so handy with tools and wood and fixing things."

"Been doing carpentry since I was a boy. Know my way around a saw and some nails, I'd say."

"You're a life saver. Come on into the kitchen and let me get you two something to drink."

After pouring three glasses of sun tea and setting out a plate of Betty's cookies from Grandma's Cookie Cutter, I wrangled my beasts into the living room and tossed them fresh rawhides to keep them busy.

"That's not how you make sauce," Elaina said, watching me get all of my Italian seasonings out of the cupboard. "Let me do it. You sit with Dan. I know how to feed a man." She pushed me aside and winked at Old Dan. He muttered something under his breath and took a sip of tea.

43

"Looks like you've got an admirer," I said, taking a butterscotch chip oatmeal cookie from the plate.

"Ever since we were wet behind the ears, that one's been tryin' to dig her claws into me."

"Well, you're both single now. Widow and widower. It's nice to have a friend to do things with, I would think."

"Suppose so. She does make a nice pot roast, too. That ain't a half-bad reason."

"More than any reason Ben has to hang around me." I laughed, but Old Dan wasn't fooled.

He took my hand and patted it. "Rough times come, rough times go. Nobody's perfect."

I hadn't heard from Ben since he dismissed me the night before. Mom came home around midnight, glowing like Audrey Hepburn in *Roman Holiday*. Dan was right, nobody's perfect, but I couldn't look at her, not knowing she'd kept such a huge secret from me. It was the hardest thing I'd ever done to pretend I didn't know what was going on, and it would be impossible not to blow up and remain civil when the topic finally surfaced.

Admittedly, Mom and Dad's divorce *was* a lot to handle on top of what was going on with Ben and me, on top of finding another murder victim.

On top of planning Canal Days.

On top of Andy being in jail.

So maybe Monica was right. Maybe she and Mom were looking out for my best interest by not telling me. But for a year?

"Earth to Cameron!" Elaina shouted, waving a wooden spoon in my face. "Gracious, Grandma Diggity is not getting any younger here. Do you have real butter or just that plastic-flavored margarine?"

"In the vegetable crisper," I said. "It's the only empty spot I ever have."

"The whole fridge is empty!" she said, swinging the door open. "How about an onion?"

"Look under the sink?"

"Under the sink? With the borax?"

"Borax?"

She wagged a finger in my direction. "Your mama and I have to have a talk."

Was that supposed to be a threat? Was I going to be grounded for keeping my onions under the sink? Mom was getting a second tour of Hilltop Castle and a complimentary chicken dinner at the Cornerstone, anyway, so Elaina would have to wait to get her word in. "Can I help you with that?" I asked.

"I don't need help. All I gotta do is toss a stick of butter, an onion, and a jar of tomatoes into the pot and let it simmer."

"What about the garlic and oregano? Basil?"

"You want to taste the tomatoes or not?"

At least she wasn't smearing the sauce into polka dots all over my kitchen walls.

Not yet, anyway.

"Sounds perfect," I said, watching Dan gum his way through a cookie. The precious old man had all of three teeth in his head. It didn't seem to stop him from enjoying Betty's butterscotch oatmeal cookies, though.

Through the French doors, I saw my sister trod onto the patio hefting grocery bags.

"Monica's back from the store. I'm going to help her bring the groceries inside."

"Now, you sit," Dan said, putting a hand on my shoulder and using it to balance as he stood from his chair. "I'll bring in those bags. Then I'll take a look in that shed of yours to see what tools you have and what I'll need to bring of my own. You ladies can sit and chat a while."

"Really, it's no trouble." The last thing I needed was the town's patriarch breaking a hip on my patio. "Monica and I can handle it."

"Won't hear of it." He hobbled out the back door faster than I could have imagined him being able to hobble. Gus and the boys were on his trail, the four of them using his exit as an escape into the backyard.

I heard Monica exchange greetings with Old Dan before she shoved the dogs aside and made her way into the kitchen. "What a nice surprise," she said, setting the bags on the counter. "Are you cooking, Mrs. Nelson?"

"That's Grandma Diggity to you," Elaina said, waggling her wooden spoon again, this time covered in tomato sauce, which flung across the room.

Monica let out a choked laugh. "Grandma Diggity? Well, okay. I'll have to come up with a catchy name, too."

"I've got you covered!" she said, flinging sauce a second time. "Diggity Cripps!"

"Diggity Cripps?" Monica and I said at the same time.

Monica wrinkled her nose. "Sounds like British chips."

"I don't know," I said, easing the spoon out of Elaina's hand and steering her toward the table and her iced tea. "It has a ring to it."

Elaina grabbed a pile of cookies and sat down. "It's young and hip!"

"You're lucky she's sitting," I whispered to Monica, "or you'd get the butt shake."

"If I'm Diggity Cripps, what does that make you?" Monica asked, pulling a bunch of bananas from a bag.

"Sister Diggity, I guess."

"You think you can get off that easily?" Monica quipped. "What are you making, Mrs. Nelson—I mean, Grandma Diggity? It smells amazing."

Elaina mumbled something through a mouth full of cookies.

"Sauce for the lasagna," I explained. "It's her special recipe."

"Oh. I thought the ricotta cheese on the list was for dog treats."

"You have Dog Diggity brain," I said. "I guess we can have spaghetti and you can use the ricotta for your dog treats."

"Good Luck Chuck," Elaina muttered, absently. "It makes their coat shiny."

"What does?" Monica asked.

"Ricotta cheese. Makes dogs' coats shiny."

I'd never heard that, but what did I know?

"Or maybe that's tuna and cats," she mused, stuffing another cookie in her mouth. "I used to have a cat."

"So I hear." I resisted the urge to laugh. Old age would get me one day, too, if I was lucky.

Old Dan stumbled in the door, arms laden with grocery bags. "Big one got a bag," he said, breathing hard.

"Big one? The dogs?" I hurried to the door and looked out to find a broken grocery bag, food all over the ground, and Gus in a tug o' war with Fiddle and Faddle, the twin trouble makers Little Liam jumped up and down yipping like a demented cheerleader, egging them on. The victim of their battle? My brisket.

"Stop that!" I yelled, stomping across the patio. Gus saw me coming and his eyes grew wide. With one hard yank, he had the brisket and was galloping across the yard with it, the twin tornados giving chase.

Exasperated, I gathered up the few other items that had been inside the broken bag. Liam challenged me for a pack of hot dogs, but proved to be no match for me.

Back inside, Monica was boiling a pot of water for pasta. "Mom's joining us for dinner. She just called. She's on her way."

"What about the Cornerstone?"

Monica bit the inside of her cheek, trying not to grin. "Apparently, Mom feels the same way I do about the Cornerstone's chicken."

"Too much pepper," I said. "You two are crazy. It's the best fried chicken I've ever eaten."

At the table, Elaina and Old Dan were debating about something. "That big one would outrun either of those other 'uns," Dan said.

"Not Chuck," Elaina said.

What was with her and this Chuck person? Wait a minute... "Mrs. Nelson, is Chuck your cat's name?"

"My cat? Heavens no! Chuck's a dog's name. Who would name a cat Chuck?"

"You have a cat?" Monica asked.

"Don't ask," I mouthed, making the universal sign for zipping my lips.

"I guess I do," Elaina said, shrugging. "I always thought I was a dog person."

"I doubt you'd forget you had one," I said, refilling her tea.

The front door opened and Mom came in. "It smells divine! Is that pasta sauce I smell?"

For a split second, I forgot about her deception. Then it hit me like a baseball bat. This was going to leave a bruise that would ache for quite a while.

She breezed in and gave everyone air kisses before coming to me and taking me by my shoulders. "Cam, I have great news." She glanced over her shoulder at Dan and Elaina, making sure they weren't giving us much attention before lowering her voice and continuing. "I got you an in with Fiona Stein to find out more about Phillis Landow."

"What do you mean?" I asked, getting an uneasy feeling about this.

"Did you know they give music lessons in the back of the train station? Fiona teaches clarinet. I signed you up for classes. You start in the morning."

I blinked a few times. "I'm sorry," I said. "I think I misheard you."

"You didn't mishear anything. Clarinet lessons. Tomorrow morning. Nine o'clock. Take your honey-sweet attitude with you."

I was still searching for my honey-sweet attitude. The last time I spent time with Fiona Stein—outside of the Daughters of Metamora meeting when they socked me with a fine—was when I fell flat on my hoop-skirted rear during a Civil War re-enactors' dinner. Not my finest hour.

Who was I kidding? That was better than being dragged into the muddy canal by my brood of hairy beasts—twice.

"Mom, I can't go to a clarinet lesson tomorrow morning."

"Sure you can!"

"No, I can't."

She batted her eyes at me, dismayed. "Why not?"

"A) I have to work. Canal Days is less than a week away. And 2) I'm tone deaf. You know this about me. I can't sing 'Jingle Bells,' let alone play an instrument."

"Psh!" She waved my arguments aside. "Work can wait an hour. You get a break, don't you? And that's what lessons are for! You'll learn! Don't be so negative, Cameron."

"But I don't even have a clarinet!"

"No worries, dear. I bought you one. Fiona will have it for you tomorrow."

"Great. You've taken care of everything."

"What have you done without me?" She kissed my cheek. An actual kiss, not her usual near-miss kiss. "It's so nice to be here with both of you girls."

"It's nice having you here," I said. Even though it had been roughly twenty-four hours and she was already running my life.

Suddenly, I was back in high school again.

· Six ·

$\mathcal{I}$ held the reed between my lips, softening it before clamping it onto the mouthpiece of the clarinet. Fiona circled my metal folding chair, eyeing me like a predator. Hair pulled back in a bun, with sharp, eagle eyes, she reminded me of an old schoolmarm. I was afraid she'd pull out a ruler and whack me with it.

"It was so surprising when your mother told me you were interested in learning to play clarinet," she said, coming around to stand in front of me. "You'd never given any indication in the years you've been living here."

"It's taken me a while to get settled in and comfortable," I said. "Now seemed like a good time to take up an instrument."

Even to my ears, it sounded like a stretch.

She nodded slowly, eyeing me. I couldn't tell what she was thinking, but it couldn't be good. "Put the reed in place and let's get started," she said.

I managed to get the reed secured like she'd shown me, and sat on the edge of my chair with the clarinet in both hands. Fiona sat beside me with her own clarinet and showed me where to place my fingers and thumbs. "The first thing I want you to do is blow into your instrument," she said. "Try to make sound and not squeaks. Place the tip of the mouthpiece behind your front teeth, place the tip of your tongue on the reed and blow a steady stream of air through it."

I did as she said and blew. A high-pitched screech wailed from my clarinet. "Let me try again," I said, sheepishly.

I blew. My clarinet was possessed. A howling, shrill banshee cry echoed through the tiny train depot. We were set up in the back of the building, where folding tables displayed ancient musical instruments and the walls were adorned with photographs from historical times in the town. It was a museum, of sorts, of Metamora's history.

Fiona squeezed her eyes closed. "You need a more controlled release of air. This isn't blowing up a balloon, it's playing an instrument. Try again."

I tried again, and got a dull, breathy note, that reminded me of knocking on a hollow gourd. A kind of thud that turned into a squeal.

"You're getting there," she said, looking toward the front of the station as a man walked in. "I'll be back. Keep going."

I was able to make a few toots and a lot more whistles and squeaks before she returned. "Well, that's enough for today," she said. "Practice at home. I'll see you tomorrow morning. Same time. Call if you need to cancel."

She sounded hopeful that I'd cancel. "Practice blowing into the horn?" I asked. Seemed like she should teach me a few notes at least.

"You can't run before you walk, can you? When you get to the point where your instrument isn't making keening death knells, we'll move on."

Keening death knells? I wasn't that bad, was I?

Remembering my true purpose for taking lessons, I smiled. "Thank you for teaching me. I'll practice every day."

I shot her a bright smile. I needed to practice keeping my expressions in check, too. Normally, they showed every thought and feeling that zinged through my head. If I was going to play nice, I needed to train my face to play nice and not give me away.

I packed up my clarinet and stepped outside, thankful that I'd made it through my first half-hour lesson. One hour a week wouldn't kill me after all.

Across the bridge, in the grassy park area where the playground and gazebo stood, I spied Ben and his dog, Brutus, with the stranger Monica spotted on Saturday with the big gray dog. The two men and their best canine friends stood facing each other. The tall man with dark wavy hair turned to his dog and gave a command. The dog sprinted to the gazebo, ran around it once, then darted inside, sniffing around like he was searching for something. The man called out, and the dog ran back and sat at his side.

I'd never seen such an obedient animal in my entire life. Not that I was an expert, but I was amazed.

As I neared, I lifted a hand in greeting. Ben saw me and waved me over. "Cam, this is Quinn Kelly and his dog, Conan. Quinn, this is my wife … umm …"

I was still his wife, even if we weren't living under the same roof. Did he feel doubtful that I'd want him introducing me as such? "Cameron," I said, holding out my hand to shake Quinn's. "That's an enormous dog." Brutus and Gus were the largest dogs I'd ever been around. Conan was a few heads taller than both.

"He's an Irish Wolfhound," Quinn said. "Ex K9 unit. He's my training partner."

"K9, as in police dog? I thought police dogs were all German Shepards?"

"They are, for the most part. Some are Labradors or Springer Spaniels, even Dobermans, like Brutus."

"Brutus is a Doberman Rottweiler mix," I clarified.

"Right, well, Conan was a training dog, so he didn't do field work very often. I preferred working with him over the other breeds, so he was given an exception."

"Where are you from?" I asked. His lilting Irish accent gave away the fact that he wasn't from around here originally.

"County Cork in Ireland," he said, and laughed. "What gave me away?"

I smiled. "What brings you to Metamora of all places?" I couldn't imagine how someone from Ireland could end up here in our tiny town hidden in the trees off of Route 52 in southeast Indiana.

"Carl brought him here to train Brutus," Ben said. "He has quite a reputation in the training community. We're making Metamora One the first K9 unit."

"You? You're going to be a K9 unit? You and Brutus?" My eyes fell to his dog who was salivating over the nearby flock of ducks.

"Brutus will be every bit as obedient and loyal as Conan when we're through," Quinn said.

"How long are you staying? Forever?" I laughed. There was no way Brutus was going to be half the police dog Conan was, even if he had saved my life from a killer a few months back. He had the drive, but it was the self-discipline I questioned. And I knew a little bit about self-discipline—just ask the twenty boxes of cookies in my pantry.

Quinn grinned, probably aware of the fact that this project would take him until next summer at least. "As long as your town will have me."

"Where are you staying?"

"I'm Carl's guest at the moment," he said, "but I'm planning on taking a room at the Briar Bird Inn for my extended stay."

"What's with the case?" Ben asked, prodding my clarinet.

"I'm taking clarinet lessons from Fiona."

His brow creased and he bit his bottom lip. If he were any more confused, or ready to bust out laughing, his head would explode.

"Don't ask," I added. "My mother …"

He nodded. "Right. Well, good luck with that."

"And good luck to you and Brutus. I've got to get to work. Nice to meet you, Quinn. I'm sure I'll see you again soon."

"It's a very small town, so the chances are good," he said. "Nice meeting you, too."

I left them to their training and traipsed across the grass to the road. Overhead, thunder rumbled and fat, dark clouds loomed. My knee had been acting up lately, so I knew a storm was coming, I just hoped it didn't hold out until the weekend and Canal Days.

$$\infty$$

The Metamora Action Agency was in an uproar when I stepped onto the peeling black-and-white linoleum tiles in the church basement. "About time you graced us with your presence, Cameron Cripps-Hayman," Roy said, stalking toward me. "That mother-in-law of yours is in cahoots with your own mother."

"What does that mean?" An ominous sensation whipped around in my stomach like a tornado.

"It means they're taking over Canal Days," Johnna chimed in. "Which is fine with me; I'm too old for this anyway."

"What do you mean they're taking over? Anna, translate please."

Anna, my red-headed fireball with a brain the size of Quinn's dog, Conan, stood from her little donated school desk. "The Daughters of Metamora reassigned the tables, declined some of the vendors we had approved, and added a pageant."

"A pageant? What kind of pageant?"

Anna swallowed, keeping her composure. "They're calling it the Miss Cornstalk Pageant."

"Mia!" I said. "She and Irene cooked this up, I'm sure. But what does *my* mother have to do with it?"

"You tell us," Roy said, sinking back into his chair. "She was standing right here with Irene ten minutes ago giving us our marching orders."

Logan's eyes popped up over his laptop. "Butch Landow sold his truck and two cows in the past six months."

My mind jerked and jolted, switching gears. Logan was my roboboy. He stayed on track and didn't swerve unless specifically instructed to do so. I'd asked him for information on Butch and he was going to provide it.

"That's old news," Roy said. "Butch lost his shirt gambling and had to sell off his truck and cows to pay his debt."

"Gambling? What kind of gambling? Where? Who did he owe?" This was a solid lead.

Roy pulled his flask from a pocket inside his sports coat. "Ask that father-in-law of yours. Him and Butch, Carl, and Steve Longo pal around. I'm sure he's in it up to his eyeballs too."

"Stewart? Gambling?" It was the first I'd heard of it. I mean, fantasy football, sure, or even a trip to Vegas every couple of years, but real gambling somewhere in Metamora? "Does Ben know?"

"He's your husband," Johnna said, weaving her knitting needle around a strand of yarn. "You ask him."

"Right. Okay, well, call the vendors back who Irene canceled and tell them it was a clerical error. Apologize, and we'll find tables for them. I'll deal with her and my mother right now." I turned around to march up the stairs but spun back to face them. "And there will be *no* pageant."

"We'll see," Roy said, laughing. "We'll see." Johnna cackled along with him.

Irene was a force to be reckoned with, and so far, I didn't have a great track record when it came to standing up to her, but that was about to change. Canal Days was mine and the Action Agency's to put on. The Daughters needed to keep their grubby hands off.

I left the church and stalked toward home, tugging my cell phone out of my bag and dialing my mother. "Did you hear?" she asked, answering on the first ring. "Isn't it exciting? A pageant. We can go shopping for a pageant dress for Mia! We'll have so much fun!"

In the background, I heard Mia shout, "Steph's going to be in the pageant, too!" She sounded positively giddy.

How in the world could I rain on their parade?

"The whole town is buzzing about it," Mom added.

"They're definitely buzzing," I said, thinking of my four seniors.

"Irene's here. We have exciting news for you. When are you coming home?"

Irene was there? Exciting news? This wasn't going to be good. "Is Monica there?" I asked. She would be straight with me.

"She and that old man, Dan, are at the hardware store buying supplies to get Dog Diggity ready to open. He's going to help her with the projects Andy was doing."

"Oh! Well, that's great. I'm glad Dan can help her out." That was one concern off of my shoulders. If Monica was worried about something, it automatically piled onto me.

"I don't know," Mom said. "He's ancient. I don't trust that he can do the job a younger man would do. Besides, he doesn't seem all there—in the head."

"He's all there. He's just … eccentric."

"Like ninety percent of this town, you mean." She chuckled. "Well, at least someone is helping your sister. So, when did you say you'll be home?"

I hadn't. I was doing my best to avoid going home. "I have a few errands to run."

"What errands? I can help."

"No, no. Just … nothing big. See you soon." I hung up before she took over buying my deodorant and changing my brand of toothpaste. Somehow I'd forgotten how controlling she could be.

I detoured, going left instead of right, to see if Ben was still at the park. I didn't want him to know I was working on the Landow case, but I needed information about what type of gambling Butch was doing with Stewart.

Luckily, it had only been a half hour since I'd left him and Quinn to their training, and they were still at it. Under the guise of asking about training my own crazy mutts, I strolled over to them. "Hello again, how's it coming along?"

In answer, Brutus jumped up on me, placing his dirty paws on each of my shoulders and giving me a loud bark in the face.

"Down!" Ben commanded and gave a tug on his leash. Brutus got down, but bounded around in circles at my feet. He was way too hyper to be trained as well as Conan.

"Progress takes time," Quinn said. "We'll get there."

"Did you need something, Cam?" Ben asked, clearly irritated by both me and his dog.

"I was just wondering if I could join you with my dog, Gus. He's a Newfoundland and—"

"No," Ben said. "This is serious police business."

"Oh. Right. I understand." I was pushing it, and I knew it, but why else would I be back again, interrupting their training session?

"Newfoundlands are beautiful dogs," Quinn said. "Gentle giants."

"He's as sweet as pie," I said, "but intimidating because of his size."

"Conan's like that, too. Wouldn't hurt a fly unless I commanded him to."

"Does he have a specialty? Like drug dog, or bomb squad?"

"Search and rescue and investigation work. He can sniff out drugs or bombs."

"Wow! What's the most memorable case he's helped solve?"

"Cameron," Ben said.

"Oh, sorry. I'm taking your training time."

Quinn observed Brutus pulling at his leash to get to the ducks floating in the canal. "I think Brutus could use a break anyway. His attention is drifting."

Ben sighed. It was the annoyed, frustrated sigh he usually reserved for me.

"They're like little kids," Quinn told him. "They require a lot of patience when you train them. They don't want to do what you tell them. They want to be dogs and follow their instincts."

Ben patted Brutus's head and nodded. "He's got a stubborn streak that doesn't help."

"It'll make him a good police dog, though, once we get him to channel it."

There was a minute of silence, so I took the reins and dove back in. "Right, so you were going to tell me about the most memorable case Conan helped solve."

Quinn pushed his wavy hair back from his eyes. "There was this one case that was hard to pin down. We got reports that a jockey was doping his race horse with performance-enhancing drugs. The owner of the horse had testing done that proved the horse was clean, but the testing wouldn't catch some synthetic hormones unless they were elevated at the time he was tested. Since Conan doesn't look like your typical police dog, we let him lose and let him find his way into the barn. He sniffed out the substance hidden in a small wooden box on a shelf in the corner and brought it back to us."

"Isn't that trespassing since he's a police dog and you didn't serve a warrant?" Ben asked.

"Not if he 'wandered off.'" Quinn shrugged. "Maybe it was questionable in practice, but Conan solved the case and we helped that horse. Those drugs could've cost him his life. I couldn't live with myself knowing I didn't do everything I could to stop it from happening."

"The great horse racing caper," I said, running a hand over Conan's wiry fur. "Well done."

Realizing horse racing was a form of gambling and I had an in to ask Ben about Stewart, I took advantage of the course of conversation. "We don't have a horse track near us, do we, Ben?"

"Only about fifty minutes west of here in Shelbyville," he said.

"Oh. Have you ever been there? Did your dad ever take you there when you were growing up?"

"My dad? No, why would he?" That look was back on his face again—constipated confusion.

"I don't know, male bonding? Doesn't he like gambling?" I asked. This was a rabbit trail, but he was following me down it, so I wasn't stopping.

"Occasionally, I guess." He eyed me suspiciously, then cut his gaze to Quinn. He wouldn't ask me what I was up to in front of a guest to our town.

A horn beeped, blessedly ending the conversation that was becoming pointless other than putting questions in Ben's head.

I turned to find Monica hanging out of the window of Old Dan's pickup truck. "That's a beautiful dog!" she called to Quinn. "Hi, Cam! Hi, Ben!"

"Hi, Monica, Old Dan." Ben lifted a hand to wave.

"Let me introduce you to my sister and the oldest resident of Metamora," I said, leading Quinn and Conan toward the pickup. Ben and Brutus trailed along behind us.

Monica hopped out of the cab, and Old Dan leaned toward the passenger window. "This is Quinn Kelly," I told them. "He's from Ireland. And this is Conan, his dog."

My sister gazed into Quinn Kelly's eyes and I swear her feet floated off the ground. Her eyes gleamed and I'd never seen a brighter smile grace her lips.

I looked at Quinn and it was obvious that the attraction was reciprocal.

I snapped my eyes to Ben and nudged him. "What?" he asked, breaking the spell and pulling all three pairs of eyes to him.

"You did it again," I said. When would he learn that me giving him an inconspicuous nudge meant he needed to pay attention to what was going on around him? Would he never catch on to my signals? Some husband! Some *cop*!

"Did what?"

"Nothing. Forget it."

"Hi, I'm Monica, Cameron's sister." She held out her hand and Quinn took it. They shook, but I noticed he let the handshake linger, not letting go right away.

"Very nice to meet you, Monica," he said. "Do you like dogs, then?"

"Love them! My shop, Dog Diggity, opens this weekend. We sell dog treats. You should bring Conan by."

"Really? A shop. That's fantastic. Congratulations. Do you have a dog of your own?"

"Well, kind of. I—"

"Yes," I said, jumping in. "She has a German Shepard. Isobel. A rescue."

"A rescue," he said, and I interrupted, and kept adding on to Monica's saintliness.

"She's elderly, too, and Monica is so patient with her."

"Rescuing elderly dogs is so important," Quinn said. "I hate thinking of them spending their last days in a shelter. I've always wanted to have a rescue for elderly dogs to do my part in making sure the ones under my care are treated with respect and dignity at the end of their lives."

I could picture cartoon hearts emanating from Monica. Even the persistent thunder overhead couldn't dampen her enthusiasm.

"Mighty hot out today," Old Dan said. "Why don't you two boys bring those dogs and come back to Ellsworth house for a cold drink?"

Old Dan gave me a wink. At least someone besides me was detecting the signals. "That's a great idea!" I said. "You can meet Monica's dog, Isobel, and my four. Ben, you can introduce Quinn to Mia, and both of our moms are there. Since he'll be staying a while, it'll be nice to get to know some other people in town."

Ben's brow furrowed for the hundredth time in the past hour. "My mom's there? With yours? Why?"

"Exactly," I said.

"A cold mineral sounds great," Quinn said. "It's fierce warm today."

Monica giggled like a school girl at his Irish lingo. "Great, we'll see you in a little while then?"

"Aw, sure look it," he said, making her blush and giggle even more.

It seemed that when Quinn was dazed by my sister his firm grasp on American English slipped, letting the commonly used Irish words and phrases slip through. I didn't think he even realized it.

Love was in the air.

Thunder cracked.

And storm clouds, I amended. Love and storm clouds.

· Seven ·

$\mathcal{M}$onica and Quinn sat outside on the patio drinking minerals, as he put it, the Irish term for what we call pop here in the Midwest. Conan, Brutus, Gus, Isobel, Mike & Ike (names I was tossing around for the twins), and tiny Liam were running around the backyard barking and howling like a pack of wild dingos in the Outback.

"How much money do you think he makes?" Mom asked, sidling up beside me behind the kitchen window curtain where I was spying.

"She can fall in love without money factoring into it."

Mom pursed her lips, like she had a terrible taste in her mouth. "It's hard to eat love, or to live in it."

"She's a businesswoman with her own shop. She doesn't need him to provide for her."

"The shop isn't even open yet. It's a little early to proclaim it a financial success."

"They met two seconds ago. It's a little early to proclaim it a failure."

"Touché," she said, spinning around and leaving my side to go back to the living room, where she and Irene had roosted with Mia and about a hundred fashion magazines. They were looking for exactly the right dress for the pageant.

I took a sip of my iced tea, proud that I could chalk up a win on life's scoreboard against my mother. Now for Irene.

"They're going to put me in the poor house," Ben said, breezing into the kitchen. "The last figure I heard was five hundred bucks. For a dress. I'm not spending five hundred bucks for a dress unless she's getting married in it." He opened the refrigerator and took out a can of Coke.

"You know this whole pageant thing wasn't even approved by the Metamora Action Agency, right? Your mother just waltzed into my office and declared herself in charge."

"So tell her it's unauthorized," he said, cracking open the can and leaning against the counter. "Unless Soapy tells her she and the Daughters are planning Canal Days, she has no authority to declare anything."

"Are you going to tell her that?"

He smirked. "Are you?"

"Is that a challenge?"

"I like getting you riled up." He took a drink from his can, waiting for my retort. If only I had one.

At some point, I had to stand up to Irene. She'd bullied and bulldozed over me since the day I moved here. My only recourse had been getting Ben to intervene. But since Ben moved out, it seemed a bit hypocritical to ask him to do my bidding, even if she *was* still my mother-in-law, and he and I *were* still married. I needed to redefine my relationship with her by standing up to her.

"Fine," I said, banging my class down on the counter for emphasis. "I'll do it."

He grinned, nodding. "Okay, but first, I have something to tell you."

"Oh no. If it's something else I need to do this week, I don't want to hear it."

"No. It's about Andy. They're not setting bail."

"What? Why not? This is crazy, Ben, and you know it!"

"I agree. There's more to it, but I haven't figured out what. For now, Andy, John, and Paul are staying behind bars."

"I can't believe this."

"I know." He put a hand on my shoulder and squeezed. "Back to standing up to my mom. You sure you want to do it with Quinn here? You want to scare him off?"

Oh, good gravy. I hadn't thought of that. "No. I don't want to scare him off." And I didn't much feel like getting into it with Irene anymore, either. Not after the news about Andy.

"Maybe you should wait until tomorrow. I bet you'll want to tell her off in the morning."

"If not, I'm sure you'll be willing to rile me up again."

"Anytime." Ben put an arm around my shoulder and jostled me good-naturedly, then kissed my head. "Let's go see if Mia has settled on a color." He groaned.

"You should've had a boy."

"Times like this, it would be simpler."

"But, she's her daddy's girl."

He squeezed me and kissed my cheek. "So are you."

We walked into the living room and Ben sat on the floor beside Mia, who was busy perusing high-end boutique websites on her laptop. Irene and Mom were flipping through glossy catalogues. They immediately scooted farther down the couch to make room for me.

"Sit," Irene said, patting the cushion beside her. "Isn't this exciting? I didn't think we'd get to do this until prom!"

Mom reached across Irene and patted my knee. "Cam, do you remember when we went shopping for your prom dress? You broke out into hives in the dressing room."

"She did not!" Irene said, and both of them broke out into laughter.

"That was when we were shopping for a wedding dress, Mom," I said. Looking back, it was kind of funny, but I wasn't in the mood to give an inch.

"It was only four years ago?" Mom asked. "It seems like it was much longer than that. Are you sure?"

"Positive."

"Doesn't seem like that long ago," Ben said. "Seems like yesterday."

Our eyes met and I knew we were both replaying our wedding day in our minds. It had been small, only close friends and family, and even if the reception wasn't the big party I'd always thought I'd have, it was perfect. It was Ben and me, and I was sure it was the beginning of our happily ever after.

"I need Monica's opinion," Mia said, standing up with her laptop and ending the moment. "I'm going to ask her what she thinks of this one."

Irene, the doting grandma, waited until Mia left the room, then said, "I'm paying for the dress. I'm so proud of the young lady she's become. I didn't see her often enough when she was little, and now I'm making up for it." She took my hand, something she's never done, and I had to resist the urge to yank it back. It was natural instinct, like pulling away when you accidentally touch a hot iron.

"You're so good to her, Cameron. I know you never expected to have her live with you on a full time basis, but since she moved here from her mother's, you've taken on the responsibility of being her stepmom and done wonderfully with her."

I opened my mouth and nothing came out, so I coughed.

Mom reached over behind Irene and nudged my hip. I could take a hint—or the meaning of a nudge. "Thank you," I managed to say through my shock.

Irene turned her gaze on Ben but continued to speak to me. "I've been hesitant to say anything due to the situation between the two of you. I was waiting to see how things shook out. Well, that and the matter of your fine. But, now that that's been settled, I think it's time." Now she turned back to me, and I was met with an expression of a queen about to bestow a great honor on a peasant. "Cameron, as a Hayman, you are entitled to take your place as a Daughter of Historical Metamora. Consider this a formal invitation of membership."

She beamed, pleased with the honor she dropped on my lap.

My heart stopped, sputtered back to life, then thudded hard in my chest. This couldn't be happening. It was my worst nightmare come true.

Ben sat slack-jawed and horror stricken, unable to even blink. He never thought he'd see the day his wife and mother became sister Daughters.

My mom rushed over to me and encircled me in an embrace, gushing. "How wonderful! What a privilege to be part of such a prestigious group of women in the community."

"Our meetings are on Sunday afternoons," Irene said, then added, "as you may recall."

Yes, I did recall my one invitation to a Sunday-afternoon Daughters meeting, when they decided to fine me for painting my house.

Mom sat back down and the three of them stared at me, expectantly. It dawned on me that I hadn't said a word—hadn't accepted, hadn't declined. Had barely breathed.

"I … uh … wow."

The patio door sprung open and Mia bounded back inside. "We're getting pizza and chips. Did you know 'chips' are fries in Ireland? How crazy is that? Fries are 'chips' and chips are 'crisps.'"

"Diggity Cripps," I mused, "like British chips."

"What?" Ben said.

They were all staring at me.

"The other day, Monica, Mrs. Nelson, and I were coming up with nicknames … oh, never mind."

But it was curious how we'd just had that conversation and it was coming up again. Sometimes the strangest ideas had common ties. Like when I was reading a mystery novel about a castle with a priceless artifact and it was like a lightbulb going off in my head, leading me to uncover Jenn Berg's murderer. Truth could be prodded out into the open by the most benign things, and being a Daughter might be one of them. This could be my link to discovering who killed Butch Landow and getting Andy out of jail.

"Irene, I'd love to join the Daughters of Metamora. Thank you for the invitation."

Even though I didn't look his direction, I heard the sigh—the famous Ben sigh of reproach. He knew as well as I did that this would open new doors for us. Or possibly Pandora's box.

$$\infty$$

Tuesday morning dawned with a hellacious racket outside my bedroom window and the dogs barking to beat the band. I clambered out of bed and fought my way past Gus and the twins to peer outside. Down below, Old Dan was hunched over a sawhorse with hammer and nails going to town. A glance at the clock showed it was 7:06 a.m. My neighbors would riot. First howling dogs and now this.

At least I had the Daughters on my side now.

Monica stumbled in. "What's going on out there?"

"Old Dan's making a bee box so they'll build a hive somewhere other than our porch columns."

"Does he have to do it the second the sun comes up?" She yawned hugely. Quinn stayed until fairly late, the two of them chattering away

67

on the patio in the moonlight. Ben and Irene had gone home, and Mom and I had made our way up to bed before he left.

Mia stuck her head inside the bedroom door. She was dressed and ready to go to school. "Why is that old man banging around in the yard this early?"

"He's fixing the bee problem," Monica said between yawns.

Mia rolled her eyes and stalked away.

I sniffed, catching a familiar scent. "Is Mom up? I smell coffee."

"And bacon," Monica said.

We followed the lure of breakfast downstairs, where Mom stood in the kitchen cooking eggs and bacon in her bathrobe. Isobel groused and growled beside the fridge, nipping at my toes when I got too close.

"Good morning girls," Mom said. "Just like old times, huh?"

I couldn't remember waking up to Mom cooking breakfast, especially on a day when all three of us, plus Dad, would be rushing around getting ready for school and work. Mornings were chaotic, a mass of rushed plans of who was picking up who from which practice or club meeting, who forgot their gym uniform and who didn't have lunch money. Breakfast was a few gulps of milk and a granola bar if there was time.

"This is nice, Mom," Monica said, pouring a mug of coffee and handing it to me.

"Really nice," I echoed, letting the dogs out. "Mia!" I called. "Come eat before you have to leave!"

A minute later she bounded down the stairs, texting on her phone with Liam scampering after her. "I have cheer practice after school, and then we can go dress shopping. Can Steph come with us?"

"I'm sorry," I said. "It's three days until the start of Canal Days. We'll go, just not today." The last thing I had time for this week was dress shopping.

"I was talking to Grandma Angela," Mia said.

Mom handed her a plate of food. "Irene and I are taking her. We know you're in the middle of the busiest week of your year. We'll handle the dress and shoes and hair appointment and everything Mia needs." She brushed a stray hair behind Mia's ear. "Such a lovely girl. There's no way you won't win."

"I need stronger coffee for this," Monica mumbled, biting into a piece of toast.

Mom was going a bit overboard with this pageant thing and sucking up to Irene, but I didn't doubt she was sincere when it came to Mia. Maybe she was just too busy with work when Monica and I were in high school, but she was turning out to be a fantastic grandma.

Irene's words came back to me from the evening before. She thought I was a good stepmom. I couldn't bake or sew. I wasn't organized. I didn't know the other moms. But somehow I was doing a good job. It was a miracle.

Watching Mia pick at her eggs with her fork and text at the same time, a surge of pride welled inside me. She might be spoiled and have an attitude, but she was also loyal and loving, smart and athletic, and like her Grandma Angela had said, she was lovely.

The phone rang. "Who's calling this early?" Monica grumbled, trying to get Isobel to budge from her spot and go outside.

Sometimes I thought my sister, like her dog, was a geriatric beast trapped inside the body of a thirty-something woman. It was no wonder she and Isobel were soul mates.

Irene's name popped up on the caller ID. Most likely, she was calling for Mia or my mom. "Good morning, Irene," I said, answering.

"Good morning, pledge," she said, her voice bubbly.

"Pledge? Am I going to have to be initiated? Are you going to haze me?"

"Initiation, yes. Hazing, not unless you deserve it!" Irene twittered like a large bird, feigning laughter.

"Are you calling for Mia? I hear there's a shopping trip this afternoon."

"Yes, we've been texting all morning about it. But I called for you."

"Oh?"

"Tomorrow afternoon, three o'clock, Daughters meeting at my house."

"This message will self-destruct—"

"What are you talking about, Cameron?"

"Nothing. Secret club meeting. Just joking around."

"We're not a secret club."

"I know. Sorry. It's early, and I haven't had any coffee yet."

"Go have your coffee, and stop being silly."

We hung up, and I realized it was the first time I'd talked to her without her telling me she was sending someone over to swipe something from my house under the pretense of every floorboard and doorknob being a precious ancestral relic.

That was progress.

Monica went outside to drink her coffee while Isobel puttered around the yard. Sue Nelson pulled into the driveway and Steph ran up to the door to fetch Mia, then they rushed off to school. Mom disappeared upstairs to take a shower, and finally, I had some peace.

Well, as much peace as a person can have at a minor construction site.

I sat at the kitchen table with my coffee and a plate of eggs and bacon. Why didn't I make breakfast every morning? I'd have to start. Maybe Monica and I could take turns.

I scooped a forkful of scrambled eggs in my mouth and the doorbell rang. My house was like Grand Central Station this morning.

Halfway down the hall, I tripped over something that hissed and clawed my leg. "Spook, where did you come from?" The mysteriously appearing cat who took up part-time residence in my house glared up at me and hissed again. I'd make it up to him later.

I secured the belt around my robe and opened the door. A man in a suit stood on my porch smiling like he was in a dental commercial. "Can I help you?" I asked.

"Good morning. Are you Mrs. Hayman?"

"Cripps-Hayman," I said. Mrs. Hayman would always be Irene to me.

"Mrs. Cripps-Hayman, I'm Arnie Rutherford. One of my clients is interested in your property. Have you ever considered selling?"

Oh good gravy. This man's name was one of the last things out of Butch Landow's mouth and here he was standing on my porch.

If ever there was a time for my bees to swarm!

· Eight ·

Jim Stein was working the ticket counter in the train depot when I arrived for my clarinet lesson. Steve Longo and Jefferson Briggs stood across from him, all three drinking coffee from the Soapy Savant and chatting up neighbors who walked by the open depot door. Jim was a boisterous, overweight man with ruddy complexion who let his wife run the show. Jefferson was an older gentleman who lived in Brookville and drove a big white Cadillac to and from his antique shop each day. Steve, the owner of Odd and Strange Metamora, was exactly the opposite of his shop—nothing odd or strange about him. Average height, average build, average looks for a man in his fifties.

"Fiona will be right with you, honey," Jim said, "go ahead back and get set up."

Since the back of the station was a whole six steps across the creaky wooden floor from the front, it didn't take long to set up my hard metal folding chair and put my clarinet together. I put the reed in my mouth to soften it and pretended not to listen to the men talk.

"Got to find somewhere else to go now," Jim was saying while scratching his stubbly chin.

"I don't want to drive an hour, though," Jefferson said. "Stew won't go that far either."

"What's going to happen to the old place, anyway? Anyone hear?" Steve asked.

"You came back," Fiona said to me, breezing out of a side door that led to who knows where.

I almost choked on my reed. "I did," I said, between coughs.

"I didn't mean to startle you." Her gaze landed on the men up front. "Don't mind them. If they don't like our noise, they can leave."

"Make all the noise you want," Jim called back to us.

"Let's hear it," Fiona said. "Blow and give me some sound. No squeaks."

Admittedly, I hadn't practiced since yesterday morning. It had been a busy twenty-four hours. But I put the clarinet in my mouth and let out a steady, strong breath of air.

Miracle of all miracles! "I did it!" I said, lifting my clarinet in victory.

"Yes. Do it again."

I licked my lips and blew into the horn again. It honked like a goose. Fiona rolled her finger in a circle, gesturing for me to keep going. I emptied my lungs, feeling the reed vibrate against my bottom lip.

To my horror, an answering honk resounded from the front of the depot. A look around Fiona showed me my partner in this duet: Metamora Mike, the resident duck who was the unofficial town mascot, and most likely born around the same time as Old Dan and Elaina Nelson.

Mike honked again, waddling farther inside, encouraged by the laughter of the coffee-swilling men at the counter.

"Well?" Fiona said. "You have a fan. Keep playing."

And so I spent the half hour blowing into my horn with Mike waddling around my chair, every now and then giving the bell of my clarinet an affectionate peck.

"I believe you've got it. Good job," Fiona said at the end of our time. "I understand I'll see you this afternoon."

She meant the Daughters meeting. "Yes. I'll be there."

"Yes, you will," she said, making it obvious she was less than on board with the idea.

If all of the Daughters didn't agree with making me a member, then why did Irene extend the invitation?

Between my brief visit from Arnie earlier and trying to decipher what Jim, Steve, and Jefferson were talking about, I didn't have room in my brain to worry about Fiona. That would have to wait for the meeting later. Right now I had to hustle over to the church and tell my seniors about my visit from real estate attorney Arnie Rutherford. Oh, and how we were going ahead with the pageant.

"Don't forget to shoo your partner out the door with you," Fiona said, eyeing Mike.

"Right." How did one wrangle a duck?

I began walking, hoping he'd follow, but his beady little eyes were shifting left and right like a criminal looking for an escape. He darted toward the back of the room, flapping his wings, and hopped up onto the table where a little train set was displayed.

"That's an antique!" Fiona screeched. "Get off! Get off!" She waved her hands, lunging at Mike. He craned his neck back and gave her a warning honk.

Oh good gravy. There had to be a way to lure him out the door. I whipped the zipper open on my handbag and dug around inside. I always had a snack inside. Goldfish crackers, cookies, something.

I pulled out a plastic pack of hand wipes, tossed them aside and dove my hand back inside. My fingers wrapped around a crinkly foil wrapper. Candy bar! Wait. Could ducks eat chocolate? I couldn't risk it. The last thing I needed was to be labeled Metamora Mike's Murderess. Shifting my wallet aside, my fingers finally landed on a sandwich bag. Dog treats. Ducks could eat crumbled dog biscuit, couldn't they?

I broke a tiny piece off and held my hand out to the flustered duck still standing on the miniature antique town.

"Don't get crumbs all over my display!" Fiona shouted.

"It's crumbs or feathers … or worse."

"Worse?"

"Let's just say you don't want your little town to look like it's suffered a mudslide."

"Oh. Oh! Get him off! Get him off!" She waved her hands around again, trying to shoo him down off the table, but he only waddled to the other end.

"It's okay," I told him, offering up the piece of biscuit. "Give this a try. I think you'll like it."

Keeping his sharp gaze on Fiona, his beak darted into my hand and he grabbed the treat. Then he hustled toward me and honked for another.

"He likes it," Fiona said. "Keep going. Get him out of here."

I held out another piece a little lower than the table. He hopped off, craned his neck and swiped it from my outstretched hand. I back up a little bit and dropped a piece on the floor, then another a little farther away, like a trail of breadcrumbs.

He didn't take them. He just stood there looking at me.

"Try picking it up," Fiona said. "I think he wants you to give it to him in your hand."

"What?" What kind of picky duck was this? I took the closest piece and held it out. Sure enough, he waddled over and scooped it up in his beak. "So that's how it's going to be, huh?" I sighed, all crouched over. My bad knee was protesting. But I had to get Mike out of here.

We were quite the sight, me duck walking backward toward the door while offering up bribery biscuits to the town legend, the spoiled canal duck who ruled the Metamora roost.

Jim, Jefferson, and Steve snickered, and I caught Jim taking a picture on his phone. "Hey!" I said. "Delete that!"

"Oh, come on now. Stewart will think this is hysterical."

"My father-in-law thinks everything I do is hysterical, this just tops the cake."

Outside, the sky was still overcast and thunder rumbled every now and again. No wonder my knee was acting up. It was like the clouds were brewing, gathering in strength and number before dumping rain on us. Every now and then the sun would fight its way through and shine a blinding ray off the canal water.

I gave Mike the last piece of dog biscuit and stretched. "Nice making music with you," I told him, and headed off across the bridge.

Ben and Quinn were back in the town green with Brutus and Conan. With no time to stop and chat, I waved on my way by and shouted hello.

Sophia House, the florist next door to the church, had pumpkins stacked on ladders, piled on hay bales, and set side-by-side inside a short, decorative white picket fence. Potted mums in white, orange, yellow, and maroon lined the sidewalk. Fall wreaths encircled each window and the door, their glossy ribbons blowing in the gentle breeze, and dried corn stalks flanked each side of the entranceway. It was gorgeous. It was fall. It was Canal Days.

My stomach clenched with anxiety. There was still so much to do.

I hurried to the church door, and jumped about ten feet in the air when Mike gave a loud honk behind me. I hadn't realized he'd followed me.

"I'm out of treats," I told him. "Go find one of your feathery ladies to hang out with. I have work to do." I left him preening his wings, rushed inside the church, and raced down the stairs into my basement office.

"There's been a development," I announced, setting my clarinet and handbag on an extra chair.

"I'd say so," Johnna replied. "My guess is a wedding by this time next year."

"My money's on spring, with a bun in the oven," Roy said. "Folks get bored and cold during the winter, find things to occupy their time, if you get my drift." He shot me a wink.

"What are you two talking about?" I asked, certain I didn't really want to know.

"Monica and Quinn Kelly," Anna said. "The whole town's talking."

"Not the whole town," Logan said from behind his laptop. "The probability of the whole town talking about anything is—"

"You know what I mean," she said, bunching her red hair up into a ponytail.

I wedged myself into my donated school desk. "They only met yesterday afternoon. Nobody knows what will happen, if anything. He's from Ireland, so my guess is they'll stay friends and keep in touch through email."

"What was your news?" Anna asked. "You said there was a development?"

"Yes." I leaned forward in my desk. "Arnie Rutherford came by my house this morning. He said he has a client interested in buying Ellsworth House. Arnie is John and Paul's real estate guy. I don't know what to do. I need to get information from him, but I never expected him to come to me."

"You have to play along," Anna said, sitting back in her kiddie desk with her arms folded. "It's the only way we'll find out how he operates."

"Apparently, his client is looking for property on the canal. Since Ellsworth House is one of the very few remaining houses still used as a residence and not a retail shop, Rutherford's clients are offering top dollar."

"Sell it," Roy said. "Sounds like a no-brainer to me. Take the money and run."

"I'm not selling my house. I couldn't even if I wanted to; it's not really mine. It belongs in the Hayman family."

"Do you think he had anything to do with what happened to Butch?" Johnna asked, winding yarn around her knitting needle.

"I don't know. Butch said his name on Andy's tape the morning he died. It has to mean something."

"Meet with him at a public place during the day," Logan said. "We can be nearby so you have witnesses if anything happens."

Anytime I included the Action Agency in a plan, there was a high likelihood of a debacle of epic proportions.

"The Soapy Savant," Anna declared. "Call him and have him meet you there tomorrow morning. We'll take a table in the corner and remain inconspicuous."

"We need a code word," Johnna said. "Like *pumpernickel*, or *rhododendron*. You can work it into a sentence and say it real loud and we'll know you need rescuing."

I couldn't imagine working *rhododendron* into a conversation at random, but I suppose it could be done.

"She needs a wire," Roy said. "Ain't gonna do us no good to get him to talk if we don't get it on tape."

"I can take care of that," Logan said.

I often wondered if Logan was a plant from the CIA. A thirty-year-old who looked like he was seventeen and got assigned undercover to our high school.

"We'll go with *rhododendron* as the code word," Johnna proclaimed.

"It's a solid plan," Anna said. "Call him and set up the meeting."

"I will. I will. I have more to tell you guys." I told them about Jim, Jefferson, and Steve talking about having to find a new place. "Do you think they were talking about gambling?"

"Who knows?" Roy said. "Ain't much to go on."

"We need an in with them," Anna said.

"We have one." Johnna pointed to Roy with her knitting needle. "This one here. All he's got to do is tell them he wants in and he'll be in."

"Really?" I asked. "Roy? Can you do that? Can you get information for us?"

"Now, it ain't that easy. Those fellas are a tight-knit group. I can try, but I ain't makin' any promises."

"Fair enough," I said. "I think we're making a lot of progress on this case. We'll have Andy, John, and Paul released in no time."

"What about your other news?" Johnna said, lowering her eyes to her needles while she worked, a small, tight grin on her lips.

"I guess the cat's out of the bag. I was invited to be a member of the Daughters of Metamora."

Anna's eyes popped open wide, and Roy smacked his leg, laughing like a loon. Logan watched them both, then told me congratulations.

"So what does this mean for Canal Days?" Anna asked. "Are they—you—who's in charge? What about the pageant?"

"Well..."

"No!" she cried, standing from her desk. "I will not be a part of planning any event that puts females on display and parades them around on a stage to be judged. It's disgusting. I can't believe you're allowing this!" She grabbed her tote bag and slung it over her shoulder. "Logan, come on!"

"Wait," I said, as Logan looked desperately from me to her and back. "Anna, it's not like that. It's—"

"It's exactly like that! All pageants are. Women are more than what's on the outside. Logan!"

He hopped up from his desk, pushing his laptop shut as she stormed up the stairs. "Uh … sorry," he said. "I drove. I'll talk to her."

I nodded, unable to speak over the giant lump in my throat. Good gravy, I'd been chastised by a seventeen-year-old. The worst part was, she had a point. What was I going to do? I'd hurt Anna's feelings if I went through with the pageant and Mia's—not to mention Irene's and my mom's—if I didn't.

∞

I sat in Soapy's office, a closet-sized space behind the area where he and Theresa made scented soaps and lotions. The aroma of the day seemed to be honeysuckle mixed with something minty. Maybe it was eucalyptus.

"So how's it coming along?" Soapy asked, flipping through a notepad where he'd jotted details for Canal Days.

"Good. Thursday I have a meeting with the vendors to go over any last-minute needs they might have."

"And are the booths on schedule with Andy indisposed?"

"The booths? What booths?" I flipped through my own notes to see what I missed.

"I thought I told you about this," he said. "Some of the town attractions, like Odd and Strange, and the train depot, and the canal boat, and of course, the Daughters, wanted display booths instead of tents and tables. I asked Andy to build them."

"Display booths? Andy?" This was news to me. My head was spinning. It was Tuesday and Canal Days started on Friday afternoon.

"I'm sorry, Cam, it must've slipped my mind." Soapy sat back in his chair and scratched his beard. "Well, this town has no shortage of wood workers. I'm sure I can pull a team of people together to get it done, but I'll need someone to be in charge. I'm way too busy to oversee booth building."

A thought hammered itself into my brain. "Old Dan! He's a great carpenter. He's been helping me by building a bee box."

"A bee box? I thought you got rid of those bees."

"They'll never leave. Dan suggested moving them to their own little luxury condo instead of my porch columns. That way maybe we can get some honey from them as rent."

He chuckled. "Good call. If you get some, put me down for a jar."

"I'll talk to Dan. He's taking over helping Monica get Dog Dignity ready, too."

"I'll put a call in to his son to see if he can help out and keep an eye on Dan. Last thing I need is for him to overexert himself."

I waited until Soapy made a note for himself.

"There's something else," I said. "I need your advice."

"What have you gotten into this time?" he asked, grinning.

"The Daughters. I believe my initiation is this afternoon."

"A little birdie told me something about that."

"Yes, well here's the thing. Irene planned a Miss Corncob … Corn Husker … Corn *Something* pageant for Canal Days. Not everyone is so thrilled about it. I need a way to include it in Canal Days, but not really include it."

He waved his hand, dismissing my concern. "I know all about the pageant. Fiona was in here telling Theresa about it. She said she was asking her son if they could use the high school gym, so it won't be downtown by the canal. Schedule it for Sunday afternoon when things die down."

"Perfect." The waves of anxiety rolled off of me, leaving me relieved. We could have the pageant for those who wanted it and not upset any apple carts at the same time. Speaking of … "We're planning on locating the farmers' market behind the shops in the grassy area in front of the horse pasture."

"What about the electric fence? I know it's normally off, but have you talked to anyone about making sure it is?"

I made a note on my pad. "No, but I'll do that today. Who owns that property?"

"Good question. I haven't heard what Butch Landow's will stated, but you might want to start with his ex-wife."

"Phillis? That's Landow Farm?"

He nodded.

"I'll find her number and give her a call." This was my in—a perfect reason to make contact with one of the main people on my suspect list. And I didn't even need to be nice to Fiona to do it. So much for honey.

And clarinet lessons.

Soapy opened his top desk drawer and pulled out an address book. "I'm the mayor. I've got everybody's phone number."

He rattled off Phillis's number, and I jotted it down. "Thanks."

"Go ahead and give her a call. I'll go make you a pumpkin spice latte. You look like you could use it."

"You read my mind. Or my face." I laughed. "Either way, that sounds wonderful. Thank you."

"Pull the door closed when you're done in here."

He left his office, and I dug my cell phone from my overstuffed handbag. My finger trembled a bit as I dialed Phillis's number, but I wouldn't let myself overthink this. For the next few minutes, she was any other citizen in Metamora whom I needed to contact about

Canal Days. Getting info about who stood to gain ownership of all the Landow land was just a bonus.

I ran my eyes over the walls of Soapy's office as a distraction while the line rang. Magazine articles about the Soapy Savant with glowing reviews of their products were framed and hung with care. Photos of him and Theresa from when they were younger and newly married were grouped in a collage on a bookshelf. They looked so young. Soapy didn't even have his beard yet.

"Hello?" Phillis answered, startling me.

"Hello! Uh, hi."

"Yes? Who is this?"

"Cameron Cripps-Hayman. I'm calling about Canal Days."

"I make sure I'm out of town for that fiasco each year, but thanks for calling."

"Wait! Don't hang up." This wasn't starting out well. "I work for Soapy. We need to speak with you or whoever has access to the electric fence that runs the length of the horse pasture behind the downtown shops."

I heard her inhale on a cigarette. "What does the fence have to do with Canal Days?"

"We're setting up the farmers' market in front of the pasture this year. We want to make sure the fence is turned off so no one gets hurt."

"This is something my ex used to handle?"

"I believe so, yes."

"You believe so, or yes?"

This was one hard-as-nails woman to deal with. "This is my first year as an organizer, but from what I understand the fence is typically turned off."

"Hmm, let me think on it and I'll get back to you. Cameron, was it?"

"Yes, Cameron Cripps-Hayman."

"A Hayman. How nice for you. Well Ms. Hayman, I have your number here on my caller ID. I'll be in touch."

And she hung up.

I took my phone from my ear and stared at it.

What in the world had just happened? I got zero answers. I didn't even know if Phillis owned the farm, or if she could make sure the fence was turned off this weekend. It was Tuesday and the vendors would set up mid-morning Friday. The festivities would begin that afternoon. I had booths to get built and a pageant to keep from becoming an enormous spectacle. All I wanted was something simple—the power turned off on a fence so nobody got zapped buying zucchini. Was that too much to ask?

· Nine ·

$\mathcal{I}$ stood at the edge of my front yard mesmerized, watching Old
Dan squeeze the bellows on a bee smoker. At my feet, Metamora
Mike twitched his tail and honked. He'd spotted me on my way
home and followed. I wasn't sure if I'd ever be able to shake him. At
least I could tell Monica her dog treats were a hit with ducks, too.

The honeybees hovered in a trance while Dan pried open one of
my porch columns. He'd cut a long rectangle along the back where,
when patched, it wouldn't be visible.

"This is one old hive," he said. "About eight years, from the size of it."

"Eight years?" That meant it had been here with Irene and Stan
for four years before Ben and I moved in. Of course she would take
the weathervane from the top of the house, but leave the bees for me.

"Hand me that scraper," he called, pointing to his toolbox. "Shoulda
put it in my pocket."

It was all fine and good for him to be close to that many bees
ready to sting to protect their territory, but I wasn't the one with a
hood on. Still, he was an old man putting his neck out to help me. I
couldn't stand there and pretend I hadn't heard him.

Could I?

I shook the question out of my head. No, of course I couldn't.

Tip-toeing across the grass, I did my best to hurry. Mike, having a strong sense of self-preservation—no wonder he'd lived so long—didn't follow. Bees flew lazily around the yard, landing heavily on the ground, like their wings were made of lead. "Will they be okay?"

"Sure they will. Smoke just calms them down. Come on now, they won't hurt cha."

I grabbed the scraper sitting on top of the jumble of tools in Dan's metal toolbox. Getting only as close as absolutely necessary, I stretched my arm as far as it would go and allow him to grasp the tool by the tip.

"Lookie here," he said, waving me over.

I eased closer and peered into the column. Sheets of honeycomb hung from the top of the column halfway down the length of the inside. "Whoa. That's enormous."

"This section of comb here," he said, tapping a whitish area, "is capped off honey." He broke off a piece. "Here, now. Taste that."

He broke a small piece off for himself and tossed it in his mouth after handing the chunk over to me. Leaning his head back, he chewed the sticky, gummy honeycomb and stared up at the sky. "That there is heaven on earth."

I'd never eaten honey straight from the comb before. It drizzled stickily between my fingers. I touched it to my tongue first. The sweet, pungent taste made my mouth water. "I've never tasted anything like this. It's so good." I took the bit of comb into my mouth. It was chewy, a little like gum, and so sweet and tangy, but with a bit of a bite.

"Goldenrod honey," Old Dan said. "That's what you get this late in the season."

He began to press the end of the scraper into the comb, cutting it straight across the top. I backed up and left the porch, giving him and the bees room to do their business. Soon he stepped away from the column holding a square of the honeycomb. He walked it down the porch stairs, slow and careful, and picked up a board of the same size.

"What are you doing?" I asked. I'd never seen anything like this before. My curiosity was piqued.

"Might as well use their own comb in the new hive. There's enough of it."

He fit the piece of honeycomb to the square board and slid it vertically into the bee box. "How many boards like that go in the box?" I asked.

"Quite a few. This will get them started. They'll have that box full of comb in no time. Best make sure they brood, though."

"Brood?"

"The queen has to lay eggs for the hive to thrive."

"What does that involve?" I asked. The last thing I needed was a hive of testy bees to babysit.

"Your mama never gave you the birds and bees talk?"

"She most certainly did," Mom said, coming around from the back of the house, jingling her car keys with Mia in tow. "We're off, and we're not returning without a dress."

"Women on a mission," I said. "Have fun. Text me pictures when you try them on."

"Why?" Mia asked, cocking her head at me. "You and I never like the same things."

"Sometimes we do," I said, but I knew she was right. Our taste and style were polar opposites. I was certain it was our age difference, but proof would be what Mom and Irene thought of the dresses Mia picked out.

"Whatever." She got in Mom's car and slammed the door.

"She's always so happy," I said, to no one imparticular.

"Hormones," Dan said.

I wasn't sure if we were talking about Mia or brooding bees, so I let the comment slide.

"Go inside and help Monica," Mom said, getting in her car. "She's got hundreds of dog treats to bake before Friday."

Monica wanted her treats to be as fresh as possible, so she put off baking for as long as she could. Betty was baking cookies for the Grandma's Cookie Cutter Canal Days table, so Monica couldn't borrow her oven. The commercial-sized one we'd ordered for Dog Diggity wouldn't be installed for another week. I could only imagine the condition my kitchen was in.

"Go on," Dan said. "Listen to your ma."

I didn't really want to leave him outside on his own to coax a million bees into a box. What if they turned on him and started a stinging frenzy? Did honey bees do that, or was that the Africanized bees I heard about on the news? How did one tell the difference anyway?

"Get," he said, shooing me away.

"Well, alright. Yell if you need me."

With deliberate steps onto the porch and past the column where the bees were coming out of their stupor and investigating their cut-apart hive, I turned the doorknob and rushed in the house.

To a cloud of smoke.

At first I thought I'd tripped over the bee smoker and brought a hazy smog inside with me, but I quickly realized my sister was trying to set my kitchen on fire.

"Monica?" I darted down the hall into the kitchen. Monica was sobbing. The fire detector started blaring, and the dogs began barking like their tails were ablaze. "Out!" I shouted, opening the back door. "Gus! Isobel! Liam!" I chased them outside while the burly twins chased each other around the dining room having a competition of who could howl the loudest. "Wally! Beaver! Let's go! Outside!" I really needed to find names for these two hooligans and stick to them.

I left the door open, ran to the window over the sink, and pushed it up as high as it would go. "It's okay," I told Monica, my eye catching the charred dog biscuits sitting on top of the stove. "I'll help you get as many as you need baked before Friday."

"Why did I ever think I could do this?" she wailed, swiping her hands across her wet cheeks.

"Because you can. Tell me one time you've failed at anything." I crossed the kitchen and stood in front of her. "You were popular in high school, college was a breeze for you, and you've been a successful businesswoman since the day you got your first job. This is new. It's challenging you, but I see the glimmer in your eyes whenever you talk about Dog Diggity. It's worth the struggle."

"Cam, my store isn't anywhere near ready to open this weekend as planned, there's no way I'm going to be able to bake forty dozen treats as planned, and—"

"And sometimes life doesn't go as planned. Change your plan. You can do this, Mon. I have no doubt in my mind."

She sniffed and gave me a shaky smile, looping her wavy hair back behind her ears. "Okay. I'll take those charcoal lumps out to the trash and we can get started on a new batch."

"*That* sounds like a plan."

∞

I was up to my ears in dog biscuit dough when the phone rang. I glanced over at the caller ID and cringed. Irene.

After wiping my pinkie finger on my apron, I jabbed the speaker button on the phone. "Hello, Irene."

"Where, pray tell, are you?"

Pray tell? This sounded serious. "In my kitchen helping Monica make forty dozen dog treats for this weekend. Where, pray tell, are you? Did Mia find a dress?"

"She did. And she's here. As is your mother. You, however, are not."

I took a moment and tracked back through my mind, trying to figure out what she was talking about. Then it hit me. "The Daughters meeting! What time is it?"

"Three seventeen. You're late."

"Oh, good gravy. I'm sorry Irene. I've got Old Dan playing with a beehive in my front yard, a hysterical sister in my kitchen, and—"

"And the Daughters are a priority for its members," she said. "If you aren't going to take this seriously, then I've made a grave mistake asking you to join."

"No, I just—I'm sorry, Irene, this week has gotten away from me. There's a million things to do. Give me ten minutes and I'll be there."

"Fine, but know that we don't always give second chances."

"Noted. See you soon." I hung up with my pinkie and turned to the sink to wash the goop from my hands. "I have to go," I told Monica. "I forgot about my first Daughters meeting."

"I heard."

"I'll be back as soon as I can to help you knock these out."

"You didn't sign up for Dog Diggity," she said. "I did. Now I have to find a way to make it happen. Go to your meeting, and don't worry about me."

Her declaration made me worry even more. "I'm abandoning you in a time of need," I said. "What kind of sister does that?"

"A sister who's a Daughter," she said then laughed. "That sounds so strange."

"The Daughters of Metamora isn't something I ever wanted. I'm going to decline Irene's invitation to join."

Monica's eyebrows shot up. "She'll make you regret it."

"She makes me regret everything. Oh, I forgot to tell you, dogs aren't the only ones who love your treats. It seems ducks take quite a liking to them, too." I told her the story of Mike following me around town as I cleaned my hands. Then I grabbed my bag and took off for my first—and hopefully last—Daughters of Historical Metamora meeting.

∞

The Daughters were all waiting in Irene's living room. Fiona was pacing back and forth like she was wound up and ready to pounce. Elaina was telling knock-knock jokes that made no sense. Cass was playing a game on her cell phone. Her eyes were still puffy and she looked like she'd lost weight in the few days since Andy's arrest. Mia and Stephanie were whispering in the corner, and Betty was nodding off in one of Irene's antique wingback chairs. Poor Betty had a million cookies to make and took time out of her busy schedule to be here. Was it because she truly wanted to, or because everyone was afraid of Irene?

"Let's bring this meeting to order," Fiona said, as the Sergeant At Arms.

Irene and my mother breezed in from the kitchen. Mom came over and tugged me down beside her on the loveseat. "I raised you to be on time. Are you using a planner?" she whispered.

A planner? If I had one, it was buried in my handbag or a kitchen drawer. I definitely wasn't *using* one.

"You need to get organized," she said. "You're running around this town like a chicken with its head cut off. That's not the Cripps' way. *Or* the Haymans'."

Oh Lordy, Irene got her hooks into Mom's brain. I was doomed. And then I noticed her shoes. Sensible flats. "What are those?" I pointed to her foot.

"Irene picked them out. Aren't they cute? I'm getting too old for those heels I wear, and these are so comfortable and stylish."

Yep, I was completely doomed.

Irene stood in the front of the room. "Thank you all for your attendance this afternoon, Daughters. This isn't our regular meeting, so we won't be having roll call, old business, or new business. Today is a special day for me, as I present—for the first time ever—a non-legacy candidate for initiation. You all know I have one son. He's always been the light of my life, as is my granddaughter, Mia. Mia will carry on our family bloodline in the Daughters of Historical Metamora, but it pleases me to present to you today a second candidate for membership from our family. Cameron, my daughter-in-law."

Irene beamed. I'd never seen her so happy. In a million years I wouldn't have guessed that making me a Daughter would give her so much joy.

Mom patted my leg excitedly. She glowed with pride. These two women were putting a whole lot of stock behind this girls club. I wished I had half of their enthusiasm for it. No way could I back down now.

"Cameron," Irene said, "please stand and take the initiate's oath of membership."

I stood. My legs wobbled. Judy Platt, Cass's mom, walked to the front of the room. "Please raise your right hand," she said, "and repeat after me."

I wiped my sweaty hand on my pants before raising it.

"I, Cameron Hayman, an ancestor-by-marriage of Elijah Levinsworth Ellsworth—"

"I …" The word came out a squeak. My breath became shallow. My head got dizzy. "I … I can't do this." I dropped my hand. "I'm sorry, Irene, everybody." I looked around the room to all of the stunned faces. "I'm honored to be asked, I really am. Right now I have so much going on. With Canal Days and the Metamora Action Agency, with Ben, with my sister and Dog Diggity, with my dogs and keeping up Ellsworth house. I barely have time to think. I won't be able to commit the time and attention to the Daughters like I should."

Irene had a very familiar expression on her face. It was one she shared with her son. The creased brow and thunderous eyes when Ben was ready to throttle me. "I'm sorry, Irene," I said. "I should've thought this through more before accepting your invitation. I'm honored, really honored. Maybe next year?"

Her stormy eyes grew wider. If she could shoot lightning from them and strike me down, she would've. "This will be your one opportunity to join us," she said, cooly. "Think carefully."

It sounded like a threat, and I was certain it was. The Daughters ruled this town. Irene had already bullied her way into fining me for painting Ellsworth house a color she didn't like, and then there was demanding a pageant for Canal Days. Those examples were only about one-fiftieth of her power on display. I had no doubt that she would make me regret this decision.

"I was late today for my own initiation," I said. "It's not fair to any of you to make me a member when I can't promise to be one hundred percent involved, is it?"

"So promise to be one hundred percent involved," Fiona said, standing shoulder-to-shoulder with Irene and glaring at me.

"I can't. There are too many other people and projects I have committed to right now. If it can't be later, like next year, then I guess it's going to have to be never. I'm sorry."

My eyes met Cass's. *You will be,* she silently mouthed from across the room. She knew as well as I did that Irene wouldn't take this rejection gracefully. I was in for it.

In the corner, Mia stood smirking. This was like her very own episode of *Keeping Up with the Kardashians.* The Hayman version, with less lipstick but all the drama.

Irene nodded to Fiona, who cleared her throat and stepped forward. "This meeting is now adjourned."

"I'm so embarrassed!" Mom hissed. "How could you humiliate Irene like that?"

"What about being honest?" I asked.

"What about being nice?" Mom sat up straight, looking all huffy and put out.

"It was the right thing to do, Mom. I can't take an oath that I know I can't keep."

My phone chimed with a text. I dug it out of my bag and saw the text was from Mia.

THAT WAS HYSTERICAL.

I replied, I'M LEAVING. ARE YOU COMING WITH ME?

AND MAKE G'MA IRENE MAD AT ME? NO WAY. C U L8R.

See you later. Great. Now Mia was embarrassed to be seen with me. We'd made such progress with our relationship since she'd moved in with me, too. Irene even said I was a good stepmom. Bet she'd take that compliment back now.

I stood up and swung my handbag over my shoulder. Cass hurried over to me. "I'll walk out with you."

"Are you sure?" I asked. "You'll probably be fined."

"Let them fine me," she said, hooking her arm through mine and walking with me to the door. "You're more of a sister to me than any of the Daughters have been. Oh, and you're taking me home. We need to talk."

We left the house and got into my car—well, Monica's car. I still hadn't replaced mine since Mia totaled it. "What's going on?" I asked, putting the car into reverse.

"I did some digging and have some dirt on Arnie Rutherford."

"Interesting. He showed up at my door this morning saying he has clients who want to buy my house."

"You're kidding?"

"Nope."

"Well, a quick Internet search shows he used to work for Collins Realty in Cincinnati. I drove over yesterday and talked with Mr. Collins himself. Turns out Rutherford was caught inflating property prices without telling the sellers. The sellers thought they got the asking price, and Rutherford was pocketing the overage. He got busted and spent a couple years in prison for it. Not a nice guy."

"No. Doesn't sound like it."

"Do you think John and Paul knew about it?"

I glanced over at her and detected a gleam of hopefulness in her eyes. I knew she didn't wish ill of John and Paul, she only wanted Andy released from jail. "I don't know, Cass. I'm going to call Arnie and see if he can meet with me tomorrow. I'll see what I can find out."

"Well, at least his offer gives you leverage over Irene."

"What do you mean? She knows Ben and I would never sell Ellsworth house."

"Does she?" Cass grinned "I bet, if you needed to, you could scare her into being nice to you for at least a day or two."

"That's mean," I said, grinning back at her.

"She's mean. And now she'll be looking to get back at you."

It was true, adding one more item to this week's to do list: Avoid the wrath of Irene.

· Jen ·

After dropping Cass off at her bed-and-breakfast, Fiddle Dee Doo Inn, I got home to find Old Dan smoking a pipe and sitting in a lawn chair beside my nice new bee box. And who was settled in on the soft grass next to him? Metamora Mike. Just what I needed. My house was already overrun with animals.

Old Dan was humming, low and deep, and tapping his foot. The tune was familiar, but I couldn't figure out what it was.

"What's that you're humming?" I asked.

"'Swanee,'" he said.

"Al Jolson, right?"

He nodded and puffed on his pipe. "Honey bees have old souls."

"Do they like it when you hum along with them?"

"Gotta sing to 'em. Get more honey that way."

"Sing? I don't sing. Nobody wants me singing outside—in public."

"Then hum," he said, and started humming again.

I left him to it and went inside, where I was greeted by my tail waggers plus one. "Hello, Conan." Quinn Kelly's dog was reserved and polite as he greeted me, unlike my monsters of drooling, jumping, barking insanity. "Shake?" I said, testing him out. He immediately lifted a paw. "Good boy," I said, taking it.

Of course a dog trained for search and rescue would know how to shake. He tilted his head, appraising me with intelligent dark eyes. He could probably get *me* to do a few tricks.

I waded through the fur and scampering legs into the kitchen. Monica and Quinn both stood behind the counter, aprons on, elbow deep in dog biscuit dough. "I found a helper," Monica said, beaming.

"I guess you did. Hi, Quinn. How'd you get roped into this?" I kicked off my shoes and plopped my purse down on a kitchen chair.

"I volunteered as long as Conan gets to sample a few."

"He can sample as many as he wants," she said, grinning like a high school girl. I was glad to see her spirits were back up after burning the batch of biscuits earlier.

The oven timer beeped, and she grabbed her pot holders. "The first batch of Dogs Dig Italian Biscuits are done!"

"What's in those?" I asked, sniffing the aroma. "Cass's fresh basil, for sure."

"Basil and ricotta cheese. Basil is a good antioxidant, antiviral, and can help with arthritis. Isn't that right, Isobel?"

The old girl lifted her furry head where she lay beside the fridge, wagged her tail once, and then took up ignoring all of us again.

Monica whipped the oven door open and slid the baking sheet out. "Perfect!"

The little bones with green specks made my mouth water. "Shake some parmesan on there and give me one."

"Let's dip them in marinara," Quinn said, inhaling the heavenly scent.

"Something tells me you two are hungry," Monica said, laughing.

"Starving," I said. "The Daughters really take it out of you."

"So it's official?" she asked. "You're a member?"

"No. Long story. I'll tell you over dinner. Let's see if Judy has a table at the Briar Bird Inn. I could go for her chicken paprikash and dumplings."

"Should we wait for Mia and Mom?" Monica asked.

"We probably should." Although I didn't want any lip from either of them about the meeting.

"Hello?" Ben called, opening the front door.

"We're in here," I said, waving to him down the hallway.

"You've managed to do it again, haven't you?" he asked, sauntering toward me through the sea of fur crashing against his legs.

"What? What did I do this time?" There was no way he had any idea that the Action Agency was snooping into the Landow case.

"My mother called me."

"Oh. That." I twisted my lips.

"Hey Quinn, Monica," he said, giving them a smile and a nod.

"We're getting the story at dinner," Monica said. "You want to join us? We're just waiting for Mom and Mia to get home."

"Sure. The story might go down easier with food. Your mom's out front harassing Old Dan. She mentioned having plans tonight, and Mia's with friends. She better get home at a decent hour even if there's no school tomorrow."

My mother had plans? Probably with Carl. This was getting out of hand. She was in town for one week and spending more time with him than visiting me.

"Why isn't there school tomorrow?" I asked.

"Teacher in-service day. I thought you knew. They're off Thursday and Friday for Canal Days, too."

"No, I didn't know. They're really making a week of it." I thought I was getting the hang of this stepmom thing, but I guess not. I didn't even know Mia was off school the rest of the week.

"That's a nice bee box out there," he said. "Are you going to leave it in the front yard?"

"I'm not touching it! It stays wherever Old Dan leaves it."

He tucked his hands in his pockets and looked down at his shoes.

"What?" I said. "You don't like it there?"

"Not me. I don't care where it is as long as those bees aren't destroying our house anymore."

"Okay, then if not you, who? Irene?"

He shrugged. "Let's not talk about this right now," he whispered, slyly tilting his head toward Quinn and Monica.

I gave him a firm nod. We wouldn't fight around the two of them. Their budding relationship didn't need to be wilted by an old married couple like us arguing about Irene for the millionth time. Besides, nothing ever came from our debates. Irene would always be his mother, she would always be a bully, and she would always have the final say so when it came to Ellsworth House.

Unless…"I have to make a quick phone call before we go to dinner," I said. "Be right back."

I darted up the stairs, cringing at the sharp pain in my knee, and closed myself in my bedroom. After emptying most of the contents of my bag onto my bed, I found the business card I was searching for and dialed the number.

"Hello, this is Arnie Rutherford."

"Hi, Mr. Rutherford. This is Cameron Cripps-Hayman from Ellsworth House. I was wondering if you were available to meet me tomorrow morning at the Soapy Savant. We can talk about your client's offer over coffee."

"I'm so glad to hear from you, Cameron. How does nine o'clock sound?"

"Sounds perfect. I'll see you then."

I hung up feeling like I had a leg to stand on with my mother-in-law. I had zero intention of selling my house, but she didn't need to know that. Besides, I had to find a way to get my friends out of jail by pinning the murder on someone else, like Arnie.

∞

The Briar Bird Inn dining room wasn't too busy on a Tuesday evening, so we sat right down. Judy joined us, indulging our table with an appetizer platter of cheese and vegetables on the house. "Ready for Canal Days?" I asked her.

"I've been ready. I've got bottles of my homemade salad dressings and shakers of my secret seasoning blends all packaged and ready to sell. How about you two?" she asked Monica and me.

Monica put on a brave face even though I knew the thought of baking all of those dog treats by Friday sent her into panic mode. "We're getting there," she said.

Quinn put an arm around her shoulder. "It's only a matter of which day she'll sell out."

It was a great way of looking at it, and it made Monica smile. "Judy's the one who will be sold out fast," she said. "Wait until you try her white French dressing."

"A house specialty," Judy said, and picked up a celery stick and crunched down on it. "Irene said the Daughters are having a display booth this year instead of a table. She's ordered posters to pin on the walls and skirting for around the front."

"Good gravy," I mumbled.

They all stared at me.

"I only found out about the booths today. Andy was supposed to build them, but seeing as how he's being detained by Brookville's finest…"

"Oh, she won't be happy about not having a booth," Judy said, grimacing.

"And we all know an unhappy Irene is an unhappy everyone else in town," I said, not even trying to tamper my annoyance. "It's not like I can bust Andy out of jail."

"I'll deal with it," Ben said. "I'll get with Soapy and see what needs done. You can't be expected to take on everything with two high school kids and Roy and Johnna. That's not exactly a dream team."

"Hey, now!" I said, ready to defend my agency members. "They each bring their own strengths to the table."

He snorted. "Yeah, if you're ever in a drinking contest, Roy's your man."

"Yeah, well, you never know." At the moment I hoped he was my man to bust a gambling ring.

"Is your mother dating Carl Finch?" Judy asked.

I followed her stare to the front of the dining room, where a hostess was seating Mom and Carl. They caught sight of us, waved, and headed our direction.

"*Dating* is a strong word," I said. "She's barely divorced and only here through the weekend."

"Divorced?" Ben said. "Dating Carl?"

"It was news to me, too," I said, resisting the urge to shoot Monica a glare.

"The gang's all here," Carl said, shaking Ben's hand and patting my shoulder.

"Too bad we don't have any seats left at our table," I said, and felt Monica's toe collide with my shin.

"Nonsense." Judy got up and patted her chair. "Angela, sit here, and I'll pull up another chair for Carl."

"I'll get it, Judy," Carl said. "Just point me in the right direction."

As he dragged one of the dining chairs over from a nearby table, Ben took my hand. "I'm sorry," he whispered. "This has to be hard for you."

"It is. I mean, it will be once the world slows down enough for me to really process it."

"How's that K9 training coming along with Ben's ruffian?" Carl asked Quinn, settling himself in next to Mom.

"It'll be a long process, but Brutus is already showing promise."

"How long?" Monica asked. I detected a hint of excitement in her tone. She would want Quinn here as long as he could possibly stay.

"That's yet to be determined," he said.

"Cameron," Mom said, "why on earth didn't you have Old Dan relocate that hive out into the woods somewhere instead of your front yard?"

"He's not exactly a young man, Mom, or a bee relocation expert. Why does everyone keep bringing up the bees in my yard? Is there a problem with the bees in my yard?"

Everyone was staring at me. Whether it was Mom and Carl, or the stress of so much to still do before Canal Days began, or sitting next to Ben when our relationship was still off kilter and the two other couples at the table where clearly enamored with their new partners, I was overwhelmed and ready to snap.

"Excuse me," I said, getting up. I made my way out of the dining room and into the ladies' room.

Standing in front of the sink, I took a good look at myself in the mirror. I was exhausted and looked it. Dark, puffy circles ringed my eyes, my hair hadn't been styled in at least a week and hung lank just past my double chin with new gray strands standing out like lightning in the dark. Thanks to stress, lack of exercise, and terrible eating habits, I'd gained another five pounds.

I needed to get myself together. I needed to find a way to wrangle all the crazy people and animals in my life into shape so I could be, too. I needed the people in this town to stop getting murdered so my friends would stay out of jail.

My cell phone rang from the now-more-shallow-than-before depths of my handbag. I took a deep breath and dug in. Just because a bag has pockets for organization doesn't mean you can find things in it. If I didn't know which pocket I put something in, how did that make me more organized?

I pulled out a rectangular packet of travel tissues, cellophane wrapped cheese and peanut butter crackers, and a mini-bible Pastor Stroup gave me before upending my purse and dumping everything out on the vanity.

My cell phone clattered into the sink still ringing. I picked it up and saw Roy's name on the display. Roy had never once called me. Something was going on.

"Roy?"

"How are your crysanthemums growing?" he asked.

I pulled the phone back and checked the display again to make sure I'd read it correctly. It still said Roy "My chrysanthemums?"

"Oh, I'm sorry," he said, sounding stiff and, well, odder than normal. "They're amaryllis, aren't they?"

"Amaryllis? Roy, what in the world?"

"Poinsettia? I don't know anymore plant names! Code word, woman! Code word!"

"Oh! You're in trouble! Where are you?"

His voice came back to me muffled. Someone else was there, too—another man. They were arguing. Then there was a thud, and the sound of a trumpet.

A trumpet signaling the start of a race.

"Roy!" I shouted into the phone. "Roy!"

It was no use. He was gone.

And he was in trouble.

· Eleven ·

en would never let me out of the Briar Bird if he knew what I was up to. I peeked out the ladies' room door. He sat at our table facing me. If I tried to sneak out, there was no way he wouldn't catch me.

I let the door close and paced back and forth trying to come up with a plan. Cass! If she was around, she'd distract him for me. I sent her a quick text telling her I was in the Briar Bird restroom and needed her help. Two seconds later she was pushing through the door wiping her hands on an apron.

"That was fast!" I said, shoving my belongings back into my purse.

"I was in the kitchen helping out my mom."

"And you didn't come out to the dining room and say hello?"

"I didn't even know you were here until now! You ordered the paprikash, didn't you? You love Mom's paprikash."

"Yes, and I'm not going to get to eat it. Listen, Roy's in trouble. I need get out of here without Ben seeing me. I need a distraction."

She grabbed my upper arms. "Does this have to do with Andy? Did he find out something?"

"Maybe. I don't know. All I know is that he's at the horse track—well, I think. I need to get to Shelbyville quick."

"That's an hour drive, Cam. Nothing fast about it."

"Oh yeah. I need to borrow your car, too."

"Whatever you need if it could help Andy." She tossed me her keys. "Be careful. I've got you covered. Wait until you hear clucking, then run for it."

"Clucking?"

She was already out the door. I could only imagine what she had planned.

I kept my ears alert, waiting for the signal. It seemed to take forever. What if Roy was in danger? Big, life-threatening danger? I dragged him into his. If anything happened to him, it was on me.

I heard loud shuffling, like chairs being moved around rapidly, then Mom yelled, "Chickens!"

"Whoa!" Ben shouted.

"They're everywhere!" Monica's voice was almost drowned out by the clucking and bawking of chickens.

I darted from the bathroom, glancing into the dining room as I hit the front door. All shapes and sizes of head-bobbing poultry ran under tables, between chairs, and skirted between the legs of my shocked family and friends. There must've been a few dozen of them.

"Cass!" Judy yelled, as Cass frantically waved her apron toward the chickens looking for all the world like she was trying to wrangle them toward the back door that stood open, but only managing to send whirls of feathers into the air like a spontaneous pillow fight had broken out in the dining room.

"I left the pen open!" Cass shouted. "Sorry!" She dared a glance in my direction and winked.

Mom hopped up on her chair and held on to Carl's shoulders for dear life. Ben waddled around, hunched over, trying to herd chickens. Quinn was attempting to capture one by tossing his linen napkin over its head, while Monica used the bread crumb trail method.

Racing to Cass's car, I couldn't stop laughing. The image of my family wrangling chickens in the Briar Bird dining room would stick with me forever. I wish I had a photo for Christmas cards. I could Photoshop little Santa hats on the chickens.

I hopped behind the wheel of Cass's blue Ford Taurus and sped down the street toward Route 52 and Shelbyville.

$$\infty$$

My phone rang about a hundred times on the way to Shelbyville. I tried not to look at the display, but couldn't resist. Most of the time it was Ben. I know Cass had to tell them something about my disappearance. She wouldn't let them think I'd been abducted or that I ran off—well, technically I did run off, but not forever. Just for a couple hours. Did they know that, though? Where did they think I went?

Guilt was a powerful motivator. It had me on the road to find Roy, and it made me answer the phone the next time it rang. Thinking it was Ben again, I put my cell on speaker and said, "I swear, the chickens weren't my idea!"

"Chickens?" Johnna said. "I hadn't thought of chicken cozies, but I suppose it must get chilly in their pens during the winter."

"Wait. What?" She'd already lost me.

"The dog sweaters I'm knitting for Monica. I figure I can whip some up for chickens too if you think people will buy them."

"Honestly, I have no idea. Did you need something, Johnna? I'm kind of busy."

"You're kind of busy saving Roy's behind, aren't ya? He left a message on my answering machine blabbering about my echinacea. The old fart's brain is so saturated in booze, he'd never remember the code

107

work is *rhododendron*. When I called you and didn't get an answer, I tried Monica. She told me you disappeared from the Briar Bird, so I put two and two together and got you running off to save that old drunk's hide."

"We need a new code word." I wasn't a drunk and couldn't remember *rhododendron*.

"I'll think on it. Anyway, I've activated the troops. Logan and Anna are on their way to pick me up. Where are we headed?"

"No, no, no. No way. I can't have them in danger!"

"We'll stay in the shadows. Incognito."

"No, Johnna. I can't bring you guys into this. I don't know what I'm facing."

"Chances are that Cass was at the Briar Bird tonight. I figure she knows something about where you're headed, and you know I can wheedle it out of her."

"You're a stubborn old woman, you know that?"

She laughed, but it sounded more like a witch's cackle.

"Fine. I heard a trumpet. I think he's at the horse track in Shelbyville."

"Well, why didn't you say so to begin with? I'll call my pal Gordie and see what he knows."

"Who's Gordie?"

"A bookie. He works the horse races. If you want to make any money at the track, you go to Gordie."

I didn't want to know how Johnna was pals with a bookie, I was just glad she knew someone who might be able to help us out. "Okay, give him a call and call me right back. And keep Anna and Logan out of this!"

"Over and out," she said, leaving me wondering if she'd keep my two high schoolers out of this mess.

My jaunt west on 52 to Interstate 74 only took me forty-five minutes. Signs led me right to the Indiana Grand.

I parked in the lot and walked past the fountains to the bright lights of the building entrance. Inside, slot machines blinked and buzzed, and televisions aired the race happening on the track outside.

My phone rang. "Johnna? What did you find out?"

"Gordie's waiting for you at the end of the bar. He thinks he's spotted our lost lamb."

"I'm headed to the bar now. I can handle this, so no need for backup, okay?"

"Logan reminded me that he and Anna weren't old enough to get in, so we're setting up headquarters here at my house. We'll check in at 20:15."

I didn't know military time off hand and didn't want to do any math to figure it out, so I used her line from our last conversation. "Over and out."

Strolling through the casino, I watched the patrons load up slot machines with coins, lay down hard-earned cash on blackjack tables, and pile red and black chips on squares at the roulette tables. I'd gambled before, but limited myself to an amount I was comfortable betting. I never understood the lure of losing all of your money, but I knew so many people got in over their heads gambling. It could become an addiction, and if you owed the wrong person, it could be a very dangerous addiction.

Roy, who had an addiction problem already, shouldn't be anywhere near this place. How had I not thought this through?

I hurried to the bar and kept right on walking until I reached the end. A heavy man in his fifties wearing a newsboy-style cap sat on the end stool sipping a glass of something amber colored. "Gordie?" I asked.

"Yes, ma'am. Are you Johnna's friend?"

I nodded. "Cameron. Nice to meet you."

He shook my hand. "I hear you're looking for a friend?"

"Yes. I think he called me from here and implied that he was in trouble. His name is Roy Lancaster."

A sly grin crossed Gordie's lips. "I know the guy. Come with me."

He slid off of his stool and waddled across the casino floor. I followed in his wake, watching as he said hello and waved to several people. Gordie was the king of this world. Of course he'd know anyone new who entered his dominion.

He pushed through a door and held it open for me. We exited to the world of horse racing, walking down a sidewalk between the stands. "Your friend is in the stables," he said.

"The stables? Why is he in there?"

Gordie didn't answer, just kept walking a step ahead of me. I got the eerie feeling of following a mafia Don into his territory, and only by his grace would I be protected from his goons.

We strolled along a path that wound around behind the track. A long barn came into view. The deafening croak of frogs came from the pond on one side of the stables. One glance at the water through the cattails had me wondering how close Roy was to cement shoes and sleeping with the fishes.

Gordie knocked on the barn doors. "It's me," he called.

The doors slid open and he stepped inside, waving me in behind him.

The bright lights overhead gave the golden hay a warm glow. That, along with the earthy scent of the horses, gave me a false sense of security. Good thing my brain remembered I was standing beside the bookie king of horse racing.

Long necks careened over the stall doors, and big, dark eyes watched me pass. The stranger in their midst. I desperately wanted to reach out and pat one of the horses, but I didn't dare.

Gordie came to the last stall on the right and kicked the door open. "Here's your friend," he said.

I looked inside to find Roy passed out cold in a pile of hay. "What happened to him?"

"He drank all his money away and couldn't pay me for the losing bet he placed. I told him he had to work it off in the stables. He got halfway through mucking out this one and I found him like this."

A shovel lay beside Roy, and a bucket stood in the corner. "How much does he owe you?" I asked.

Gordie crossed his arms. "Since he's a friend of Johnna's, he owes me the rest of this stall cleaned and we'll call it even."

I knew there was no getting Roy sober enough to clean the stall, so I hooked my handbag on the stall door and rolled up my sleeves. "Okay. I'll get it done. Then I'll get him out of your hair."

Gordie tipped his hat. "Nice doing business with you, ma'am."

I sauntered across the trod-on hay to where Roy lay and nudged his leg with my foot. "Hey! Roy! Wake up!"

He muttered something and rolled over on his side facing the stall wall.

I bent down and grabbed the shovel. "You owe me *big*, mister."

The odor was pungent. Manure on a farm in the spring smelled a lot different than manure in a small enclosure. Fortunately, the stable hands kept the stalls clean, so the entire place didn't reek.

A pitchfork rested against the wall. I had no idea how to muck a stall, but figured the fork was for hey and the shovel was for the piles that were ten times larger than what even Gus left in my backyard.

I headed to the back corner, slid, grappled for something to hold on to, then lost my footing and went down hard in a slick spot in the hay-covered stall. Oh good gravy, I was sitting in horse urine.

I got back up and got busy. I wasn't planning on spending all night on this project, but it had to be done right for the horse who stayed here.

And so Gordie wouldn't put me on his hit list—if he had one.

Who was I kidding? He definitely had one.

"You want to sift through the hay with the pitch fork looking for clumps?" a very short man said, standing in the stall door.

"Thanks. I'll do that. Are you a jockey?"

"What gave it away?" he joked. "Short guy in a horse stable, right? What about you? I doubt you're one of the owners mucking a stall, and I know you don't work here."

"My friend here"—I poked Roy gently with the pitch fork—"got himself in some trouble, so I'm bailing him out. Literally, it seems."

"Is he your boyfriend?"

I almost choked. "No! Good Lord, no. We work together." I twisted the wedding ring on my finger. He must not have seen it. "I'm married."

He took his jacket off. "Let me help. You'll be here all night at the rate you're going."

"Thank you. You're a life saver. I'm Cameron—Cam."

"Buckley. Fletcher Buckley, but I go by Buckley."

"Nice to meet you," I said. "How long have you been a jockey?"

"This is my first year."

"Do you win a lot?"

He chuckled. It sounded a bit like a horse nicker. "No. My horse and I are both new to the racing circuit. We're still trying to prove ourselves."

"What's your horse's name?"

"I race Roderick's Rapid Feet of Roderick's Racers."

"Wow. That's a lot of *R*s." I laughed. "I love racehorse names. How do they come up with them?"

"Sometimes it's a combination of the breeding mare and stallion's names. Rapid Feet's mother is White Rapids out of Cedar Creek. His father is Feet of Fire, from Albany."

"Hence, Rapid Feet. That's interesting. I didn't know it had rhyme and reason to it."

"It doesn't always." He shook his head. "I know of this horse named Woobee. The owner let his four-year-old name him. That's a lot of money to spend for a horse to name him Woobee."

"How much are racehorses?" I asked, sifting through the hay. This project was coming along a lot faster now that I had someone to share the duties with and talk to.

"A yearling is about sixty-five grand."

"Holy—that's a lot!"

"Yes, it is. Racing is a big-money sport."

I jerked my chin in Roy's direction. "I think this guy just found that out."

"You can't believe how much trouble people get into betting on the races."

I rested my pitch fork tines on the ground and leaned on the handle. "I man where I live—Metamora—was murdered a few days ago. Rumor has it he was in a ton of debt from gambling and owed the wrong person."

"You think it was Gordie?" Buckley chuckled. "He's all bluster. He's never hurt a fly."

"Do you know who would hurt someone?"

He shook his head. "Nah. I steer clear of the betting scene. Everybody knows Gordie, though."

I took my inquiry a step further. "What about Butch Landow? Ever heard of him?"

"Butch? Sure. I've met Butch before. Hangs around with a couple of other fellas, Stewart and Steve."

"Then I'm sorry to tell you it was Butch who was killed."

"Really?" Buckley stopped shoveling and looked me in the eye. "I can't understand that. As far as I know he never bet on horses."

"Well, he bet on something."

"Luck wasn't on his side, I guess."

"Guess not."

So Butch would come here with my father-in-law and Steve Longo, but not bet on the races. How could that be if he was in gambling debt? What was he betting on if not horses?

· Twelve ·

My eyes popped open. The phone was ringing. It was still dark out.

After taking stock of the situation, I reached for the phone on my nightstand, glancing at the alarm clock. Half past five in the morning. No wonder Gus and the Wonder Twins hadn't budged from where they pinned me down in bed on top of the quilt. It was too early to bark and jump on the bed like birthday party kids on a trampoline.

Who in the world was calling? Then it hit me—I'd disappeared from the Briar Bird last night. After I hauled Roy home and got back to Ellsworth House, Monica was already in bed and Mom wasn't home yet. Ben would be wondering where I'd run off to. I was surprised he hadn't called in a missing person report on me. "Hello?" I answered with a croak.

"Good morning, Cameron. It's Fiona. Due to the conflict with the Daughters, I'm canceling our clarinet lessons going forward."

"Oh," I said. I kind of expected this, but I wasn't sure how I felt about it. "Thanks for calling."

She hung up without so much as a goodbye.

I put the antique phone receiver down and fell back against my pillow. Gus belly crawled up the bed beside me and rested his head on my shoulder, staring at me with his big brown eyes. "Don't worry," I told him. "I'm not that upset." I stroked his head and rubbed his ears. Who was I kidding? I'd gotten myself into another dust up— heck, a dust storm this time—with the Daughters. And the kicker? I was starting to really like playing the clarinet.

Wrestling over two hundred pounds of dogs to get out of bed, I put my feet on the chilly hardwood floor and stood, stretching. Seeing as how I'd scheduled a meeting with Arnie Rutherford at the same time as my lesson, I supposed it was a good thing Fiona canceled.

I threw on my robe and tied it as I headed down the hall with the dogs. Liam darted from the spare bedroom and joined in the parade down the stairs. I don't know what time Mom got up in the mornings, but coffee was already brewing in the kitchen. A glance out the French doors to the patio showed the sun cracking a red eye open. *Red sky in morning, sailors take warning.* The ancient rhyme and the pain in my knee were reliable sources of weather forecasting. It was going to storm soon. I hope it came and passed before Friday.

Mom sat with her coffee cup, texting on her cell phone. After pouring myself a cup, Gus, Fiddle, Faddle, and I stepped outside to join her. Liam darted down the hall and back upstairs. I knew I should grab him before he had an accident on the floor, but I needed coffee before I had enough energy to give chase.

"Look who came back," Mom said, not looking up from her phone.

"Morning. Who are you texting so early?"

"Carl," she said, with a school girl grin. "He's coming over to help me, Monica, and Quinn bake today."

Good gravy, a whole nest of lovebirds in my kitchen. "That's nice of him."

"He's a very nice man," she said, sighing.

"Yes, he is," I said. I couldn't refute the fact. Carl was an upstanding neighbor and even though Soapy was the mayor, it was like Carl was governor—if a minuscule town could have a governor. He was bigger than life. A legend in our corner of the world. Of course, you can't really build a castle on a giant hill and not become a legend.

"So where on earth did you disappear to at dinner? Not a word about leaving, you just take off? We were worried sick until Cass told us you had an Action Agency emergency to take care of."

Bless Cassandra Platt!

"Roy got himself into a situation. It was no big deal."

She shook her head. "You should never hire drunkards."

"Well, he volunteers." Plus, despite his faults, my team wouldn't be the same without him.

I noticed Isobel sitting under Mom's legs, warm, cozy, and half-hidden in the drape of her robe. That dog liked everyone but me!

"Are you having a party out here?" Monica asked, coming out to join us. "I thought I'd be the only one up this early to start mixing up bowls of dough."

"What's on the menu today?" I asked.

"Dogs Dig Honey Bones," she said. "Old Dan promised to get me a big slab of fresh honeycomb from the hive."

"Your testers are going to be happy campers today," Mom said, reaching down and scratching Isobel's neck.

"Those dogs eat better than I do," I said.

"I think Isobel has allergies." Monica reached down and took her grumpy dog's chin, turning it back and forth. "She always has crusty eyes. The raw honey should help with that. It's great for preventing allergies."

"You've really been doing your homework," I said. "Holistic dog bone remedies."

117

"If I'm going to make them treats, they might as well be good for them."

Monica would make a good mom. I'd never thought of my business-oriented sister as a family woman, but settled down in this small town, baking dog treats and loving her life, I could easily see her getting married and having a baby or two.

The thought thrilled me. I wouldn't be having a baby of my own, but Monica having one would be the next best thing. I could babysit and take the kid for strolls by the canal; we could sit on the bank and toss bread to the ducks.

If only Quinn Kelly didn't live across the Atlantic. How could my sister settle down with a man who lived thousands of miles away?

As quickly as the vision of a little Monica came into my mind, it vanished.

The sun had risen, and I figured it must be a quarter after six. "I guess I better get in the shower. Another busy day."

"You're telling me," Monica said. "Canal Days better be worth all the fuss."

"It is," I said, slipping back inside. Monica would sell out of dog treats quicker than you can say Jack Robinson. It would be the perfect introduction for Dog Diggity's opening in town.

Upstairs, Liam was whining outside of Mia's bedroom door. Just as I grabbed her doorknob and turned it, the front door opened and closed, somewhat stealthily. As stealthily as a creaky old door *can* open and close. Whipping Mia's bedroom door open, I looked around. The bed was made, and she was nowhere in sight.

"Mia!" I shouted. "Mia?"

"I'm down here!" she yelled from somewhere in the vicinity of the kitchen.

I raced back down the stairs and found her taking a yogurt out of the refrigerator. "Was that you coming inside?"

She nodded.

"Where were you? Why wasn't your bed slept in?" My mind was putting this puzzle together and was coming up with an ugly picture.

"What do you mean? I made my bed this morning and went outside to let Liam out."

Liam had been upstairs with me. The little dog scampered around her feet. "Why wasn't he sleeping in your room last night like always?" I asked, eager to catch her in her lie.

She shrugged.

Then it hit me. "You have on Stephanie's clothes!"

She rolled her eyes and plopped her yogurt cup on the counter. "Fine. I spent the night at her house, okay? I knew you'd have a hissy fit about it for no reason, so I lied."

"No, not okay! You didn't come home, didn't ask permission, and didn't even call. You're grounded! Give me your phone."

"What?" She clutched her cell phone to her chest. "No. You didn't even know I was gone!"

"Hand it over." I held out my hand, palm up.

"No! You're not my mom! You're barely my stepmom!"

Her words jabbed my heart. "I'm calling your father."

She flipped her hair, dismissing me, and stalked out of the kitchen. "Whatever."

I dialed Ben's number and got his voicemail. "We need to talk about Mia. She stayed with Steph last night and didn't tell me. She blew off my punishment. You need to do something about this. Call me."

I hung up feeling defeated.

Barely her stepmom, indeed.

A dull tapping on the front door drew my attention from my despair over Mia. I stood still and listened for it again. A few seconds later, it sounded once more.

I tip-toed down the hall, ears peeled.

Tap, tap, tap.

It wasn't a knock that a person would make on the door, and it wasn't one of the dogs. Spook the cat sneaked in silently whenever he pleased.

Slowly, I took ahold of the door handle and eased it open only to be faced with Metamora Mike and a loud *quack!*

Oh, good gravy. "What do you want?"

He quacked again, reared up, and shook his tail feathers.

"Clarinet lessons were canceled. You'll have to find someone else to harass."

He darted for me, trying to get inside. "No, no. No ducks in the house. Stay here."

I eased him away from the door and closed it. I'd made a dog treat addict out of him, and he would never leave my yard. In the kitchen, I opened the beehive–shaped treat jar Betty had given me and took out a bone-shaped biscuit.

Back at the front door, I stepped out on the front porch and sat on the step with Mike waddling around beside me. "Here you go. Is this what you want?" I broke a small piece of the biscuit and fed it to him. He gobbled it down like it was the duck version of chocolate chip cookies, which were my own food vice. "I get it," I told him. "You and I aren't so different."

My fuzzy black and yellow friends buzzed in and out of their new hive-in-a-box, landing on my potted mums and cone flowers. Overhead, dark clouds scuttled past fluffy white ones.

My mind travelled back to the night before. There was a big piece missing from what I knew about Butch Landow's gambling. What I did know was A) he was in debt and selling things, like his truck, to pay whoever he owed, 2) he hung out with Stewart and Steve Longo, who bet on the horse races, and finally, according to Buckley, Butch never bet on the horses.

So where did that leave me? Missing a key element—what did Butch lose his money betting on?

∞

Fifteen minutes before nine o'clock I walked into Soapy's and found my four seniors sitting at the back corner table joined by Elaina, now known as Grandma Diggity. To my horror and, admittedly, my amusement, she had a fake mustache perched on her upper lip. Johnna gave me an apologetic smile and shrugged. "Can't take her anywhere."

I patted Anna on the shoulder. "I'm happy you're here. I hope having the pageant at the high school instead of right where the vendors are will be an okay compromise?"

She twisted her hair around her finger and glanced at Logan. "I understand that not everyone has the same opinions about things that I have, so it's fine. As long as I don't have to help with it."

"No, of course not." I couldn't help myself and bent to give her a quick squeeze. She was a good kid with a solid head on her shoulders. "Guess I should pick a table before Arnie Rutherford gets here."

"Cameron?" Roy grasped my hand. "A word?" I nodded, and he stood and led me a few feet away. "About last night, did you find out who killed Butch?"

"You mean while you were passed out in a heap of hay and I was shoveling horse manure?"

"Let's not get testy. I said I'd gamble with that father-in-law of yours and I did. What happened in the meantime is a sacrifice I was happy to make."

"A sacrifice? I'd say you had a pretty good time last night."

"I sacrificed every last dollar in my billfold, Cameron Cripps-Hayman! Did you learn anything or not?"

I sighed. Roy would never admit he had a problem. "Unfortunately, the only thing I learned is that Butch never bet on horses, so he must've been betting on something else."

He furrowed his brow and rubbed the scruff on his chin. "Doesn't make sense," he muttered.

The bell above the door jingled, and I hurried over to a table in the center of the room. "We'll be right here," Johnna whispered rather loudly.

Arnie Rutherford sauntered up to the table in a dated three-piece suit. "Good to see you again, Mrs. Hayman," he said, extending his hand for me to shake. All I noticed was his pinkie ring, a chunk of black hills gold flashing in my eyes.

"What can I get you?" Soapy asked, coming up behind him as we shook.

"I'll have one of your caramel apple lattes," I said.

"Make it two." Arnie set his briefcase on the floor and sat down. "I was surprised to hear from you," he told me. "I didn't think you had any interest in the offer."

"It never hurts to have all the information," I said. "Is your client interested in living in Ellsworth House or using it as a commercial property?"

"Both actually. It's a prime location for my client's business interest and a lovely home."

"What is your client's business?"

"They've asked me not to divulge that information."

"That's odd. What are they hiding?" I shouldn't have asked the question. It was a natural response, but it seemed to put him on edge.

"Hiding? Nothing. They would like the offer to stand on financial merit alone."

"I'm sorry, but that's not good enough. I have friends and neighbors to think about. I wouldn't sell to just anyone."

"I can assure you that selling to my client would be just like keeping Ellsworth House in the family."

It was a strange thing to say. The entire conversation made me uneasy. There was so much below the surface that he wasn't saying for some reason.

"Do you wish to know the offer amount?" Arnie asked.

"First I'd like to know if your client is aware of the two homicides we've had in town recently. I'm surprised that anyone would want to live so close to where both of the victims were found."

"A most tragic situation. My client is fully aware of the circumstances surrounding both cases."

"And they aren't put off by having a murderer on the loose?"

"I'm confident the police have arrested the culprit."

"Which one? Andy Beaumont, John Bridgemaker, or Paul Foxtracker?"

"I can't say, but I have faith in our officers."

I leaned forward and stared him down. It was a bold move, but I had something by the tail here, I could feel it, and I wasn't letting go. "John and Paul are your clients. They were at the Landow Farm the morning Butch was killed. He wouldn't sell his farm to them for their casino. Did they kill him? Did Phillis Landow inherit the farm, and is she going to sell to them?"

He uncrossed his legs and leaned over the table, meeting me glare for glare. "You're treading into territory you know nothing about. I wouldn't go digging up dirt on that farm if I were you."

"Are you threatening me?"

"I'm warning you."

A ripple of fear shot through me at the coldness in his icy gray eyes. I no longer felt safe sitting at this table with this man, even if I was in the middle of the Soapy Savant with my friends a few yards away. He could be the murderer. He could have a gun in his briefcase.

I sat back and called out the Action Agency's secret code word. "I'm hungry. I wish they served ham on *pumpernickel* here."

My abrupt shift of topic confused him. He sat back and tilted his head. "Perhaps a pastry?"

"I really have a craving for *pumpernickel* for some reason." I pretended to scratch my ankle and glanced at the corner table. Not one of my agency members were paying one bit of attention to me. Roy and Johnna were bickering about something, and Elaina was styling Logan's hair with coffee stirrers while Anna laughed her head off. Rutherford could've hauled me out of there by my earlobes and they would be none the wiser.

"Well, Mrs. Hayman, it was … enlightening … speaking with you this morning," he said, rising from the table. "I can't help but think this meeting was your way of questioning me about Mr. Landow. Be careful. One day you just might question the wrong person."

With those menacing words of parting, he whipped his briefcase off the floor and stormed out.

"Didn't even wait for his latte," Soapy said, approaching the table with two steaming mugs.

"He was in a hurry. I'll take one to go."

He sat in the vacated chair. "What was that all about? You look like you don't know if you're coming or going."

"I don't."

"That man's a realtor, I do know that. Are you and Ben thinking of selling?"

"No. It's a long story." I tried for a reassuring smile, but being cautioned about poking my nose into something I'd regret made it hard.

Soapy reached over and patted my hand. "If you need help with anything all you need to do is ask."

I nodded, tears brimming in my eyes. My neighbors—my friends—were more supportive than they could ever realize. "I know. Thanks, Soapy."

"I do want to give you a heads up about something I saw this morning, though."

Before he rained more news I wasn't prepared for down on my head, I took a sip of the steaming, caramel sweetness, closing my eyes to savor the hot coffee hitting my stomach.

"Mia was dropped off this morning in front of the Soda Pop Shop. It was a car I'd never seen before. Cameron, it was a boy driving. They kissed before she got out."

The coffee in my gut instantly froze along with all of my extremities. "What?" I'd heard him, but it was all I could think to say.

"I'm sorry. I thought you should know. I was going to tell Ben when he stopped in for his mid-day coffee, but you came in first today."

"Lucky me."

The door jingled, and Soapy got up. "Customers." He gave me a comforting smile before leaving the table.

Mia and a boy. A boy who dropped her off this morning at Steph's house, where she changed her clothes and then came home and lied about staying overnight with her friend. Sixteen was way too young to be out all night, but add a boy into the mix and this was grounds for locking her in the house until she turned eighteen.

How in the world would I break this to Ben? He was going to lose his mind.

Being a stepmom had never been glamorous, but Mia and I had made big strides since she came to stay this past summer. This was the first major issue I'd had to face. I was in over my head. I needed an experienced mother to give me advice.

Elaina plopped down in the chair across from me. "That girl of yours has been out cattin' around," she said.

"Good gravy." I let my head fall into my hands. Did the whole town know? This wasn't the experienced mom I was hoping would help me.

"Now, I don't mean to tell you how to raise her up," she said, wagging her finger at me, "but when Sue acted up like that, I made her stand knee deep in the canal and tell everybody who walked by what she did."

That punishment sounded a bit too *Scarlet Letter* for me, but I got her drift. Severe consequences. "I think I know just how to get through to her," I said.

Mia would hate me for the rest of her life for what I was about to do, but it had to be done. She hadn't broken a little rule, or refused to do the dishes; this was major, and she'd know I meant business. This punishment was something only I had the power to do, not Ben.

Mia would know not to cross me when I told her she wasn't allowed to be in the Princess Pumpkin Pageant.

Or whatever it was called.

· Thirteen ·

Arnie's guilty as sin," Johnna said, sitting at my dining room table knitting. We'd all come back to Ellsworth House to go over what we knew about Butch's murder, which wasn't a lot.

"We have no proof of that," Roy said, taking a nip from his flask.

"It's not even noon!" Anna swiped the flask from his hand, screwed the top on, and stashed it in her backpack. "You'll get that back when we're done."

He crossed his arms, brooding.

Logan tapped on his laptop keyboard, then swiveled it around to face us. "There's a first-degree connection between Mr. Rutherford and the Mound Builders' Association," he said, pointing at the screen. "He won a lawsuit for them ten years ago when a supermarket bought a parcel of property and found an American Indian earth mound situated on it."

"Rutherford's been associated with John and Paul for ten years," Johnna said. "Big deal. That's not illegal."

"It's a connection that goes beyond this case," Logan argued.

"He did a good job and they hired him again," Johnna said, looping blue yarn around her knitting needle. "Not illegal."

"Okay," I said, "so we don't have a smoking gun. We're building a case, though. What else do we have?"

"Isn't the spouse, or ex-spouse, the first person the police usually suspect?" Anna said. "Has she been questioned?"

"I don't know," I said. "I called Phillis about turning off the electric fence for Canal Days so we could have the farmers' market there. She twisted and turned the conversation, and by the time we hung up I didn't know up from down. I still don't know if she can turn the fence off."

"I'll handle her," Johnna said, turning to the sideboard where an antique telephone sat. "What's this about a fence?"

"You know Phillis?" I asked. "Why didn't you say so?"

"Nobody ever said we were trying to get info from her!"

"I didn't?" I thought back. I guess I hadn't. I remembered discussing Phillis with Cass, Mom, Monica, even Stewart at the BBQ, but not my own Action Agency members. "I'm sorry. I've been so busy with Canal Days and my mom's visit, and—"

"And you've neglected us," Roy said.

"We know, dear," Johnna said. "You have a lot on your plate. Now be quiet so I can worm information from Phillis." She dialed the number and held the receiver to her ear.

We sat silent as stones, eyes locked on Johnna. Behind the pocket door, muted sounds of Mom, Monica, and Quinn murmuring and bowls and baking pans clinking could be heard in the kitchen. Then there was a loud giggling from outside the open dining room windows.

"Get your sticky fingers off of me, Elaina!" Old Dan bellowed.

"It's Grandma Diggity!" she called. "Come back here and have some honey!"

Roy shook his head. "The libido on that woman is astounding."

At her age it was remarkable, I had to give her that.

"Hello? Phillis, this Johnna. Are you going to turn off your fence for Canal Days or not? We're down to the wire, dear, and need to finish planning. Oh, I see. I'm sorry to hear that. Who can answer that question for me?" Johnna shot us a wink. "You don't? I thought you might know considering your close history with Butch's brother."

She shifted in her chair and picked up her knitting, weaving her yarn like she wove Phillis into a frenzy on the line. "No, of course not. I wouldn't tell a soul."

Roy put his forearm over his mouth, laughing quietly into his sleeve.

"She's good," Anna whispered to me.

"Very."

"No need to explain to me," Johnna continued. "These things happen. So, about that fence. Who owns the property now that Butch is gone? Really? It's not in probate? So who owns it then? Hmm … that's interesting. And you don't know who owns Track Times, Inc.? I see. Well, we'll make alternate plans for the farmers' market. Take care, Phillis."

We waited until Johnna finished saying goodbye and hung up before pouncing. "What did she say?" I asked.

"She doesn't own the farm. She doesn't know who it transferred to. The will named a company called Track Times."

"Track Times," Anna repeated. "Times … like a newspaper?"

"Track, like horse track, more like," Roy said. "'Cept he didn't bet on horses, now did he?"

"No," I said, my mind racing around the details. "There's something missing. Something that ties everything together."

"Good luck catchin' me," Old Dan shouted from outside.

"I can't think with that racket," Roy said.

Logan started taking notes. "We'll rope off the area."

"What area? What are you talking about, boy?" Roy asked. "You're off on another topic again, ain't ya?"

"The farmers' market," Logan said. "We'll run a rope in front of the fence."

"Right," I said. "Good idea, Logan."

"Break time," Johnna declared, standing and stretching. "I think I've earned a snack. What do you have to eat?"

I got up and opened the pocket door, and the five of us ambled into the kitchen. "They've emerged from their work," Mom said, kneading dog biscuit dough. "We could use some reinforcements."

"These troops are here for food," Roy corrected, opening my pantry.

Anna smacked his hand. "You can't just go opening people's cupboards, that's rude."

"Girlie, you're lucky I like you."

"If you're not helping, you have to get out of the kitchen!" Monica shouted. Her hair frizzed out of her pony tail, her eye makeup was smeared, and her chest heaved. This was a woman on the verge of hysteria.

"I think Old Dan could use some help," Quinn said, herding my Action Agency out of the kitchen. "I'll run and pick up some sandwiches for lunch if someone wants to come with me."

"I will," Logan said. I smiled. My introverted brainiac was eager to get out of this house of chaos.

"Conan, come!" Quinn commanded, and his dog was at his heels at the front door in two seconds flat.

Outside, they crossed the sidewalk and got into Quinn's pickup. Metamora Mike waddled after them as fast as his stubby little legs would go. He'd had enough of the rowdiness, too, apparently.

"Keep away, now." In the yard, Old Dan held a long stick between himself and Elaina.

She grinned like the devil and wiggled honey-covered fingers. "A little honey for my honey!"

"I'm not your honey. Stay back, you hear?"

I stepped off the porch and my foot landed on something that rolled underneath it. I went down hard, flat on my bottom on the last stair step. It hurt enough to bring tears to my eyes.

"Don't move," Anna said. "You might have fractured something."

"Busted her butt, you mean," Roy said, kneeling down next to me. He picked up a glass canning jar. "This is the culprit."

"They're collecting honey out of the old hive in the porch column," I said between gritted teeth.

"Looks like they're doing more than that," he said, eyeing Elaina and Old Dan.

"Help her up," Anna said, putting an arm around me.

"I'm okay," I assured her, getting to my feet. "Just needed a minute to catch my breath."

Johnna had picked up another jar and was breaking off pieces of honey comb from the column. "You don't mind if I take some, do you?"

Taking things that don't belong to her was Johnna's specialty, but I didn't mind giving her some honey. I had an overabundance after all. "Take some. All of you, take some. I've got plenty to go around."

"We should sell it," Roy said. "Get new desks for the agency. Those little kid seats are hard as rock."

"We should!" Anna grabbed another glass jar and ran up the porch steps. "I bet we could get ten dollars a jar."

"Look in here," Johnna said, standing on tip-toe. "We could get a hundred jars out of this."

"We're going to need more jars," Roy said. "I'll go get some."

"They don't have canning jars at the Cornerstone," Anna snapped.

"I wasn't going to the Cornerstone, Little Miss Sassy. Right next door here at Schoolhouse Antiques. Will has a bunch of 'em." He crossed my yard, heading for Will Atkins's antique shop. "I'll bring you a receipt, Cameron."

"Great." I hadn't given my go-ahead, but it seemed I'd be reimbursing this latest project. "I hope we can sell enough to cover the cost of the jars."

"We'll make a killing," Johnna said, scooping honey into a jar with her knitting needle.

"I'm going inside to check on Monica." I stepped over the stray metal lids on the porch, not eager to fall back down on my keister.

"She could use a nip off Roy's flask if you ask me," Johnna said.

I couldn't argue with that logic.

Inside, the house was warm from the oven and smelled sweet from the honey. Mom was placing small dog bone–shaped treats into bags. "This tray makes twenty-eight dozen," she said. "We'll make it."

Monica stood at the sink drinking water, wiping her forehead with the back of her hand. "The shop won't be ready. Frank Gardner's working on booths for Canal Days and doesn't have time to help with Dog Diggity. Old Dan can't do it on his own. He was going to go over, but I told him not to."

"That was a good idea," I said. "I'd hate to think of something happening to him over there by himself." I leaned against the counter beside her. "Don't worry. Andy will get out of jail soon and he'll have the shop finished in no time."

She shook her head. "I really hoped it would be open for this weekend. I can't believe they'd think Andy had anything to do with killing someone."

"I'm working on it," I said.

"Working on finding out the identity of a murderer?" Mom asked. "Leave that to Ben and the police. Your job is to put on Canal Days, not put yourself in danger. If you want to go into law enforcement, then you need training and a badge. Until then, I don't want to hear anymore about you playing private detective. Understand me?"

"Mom, I'm not ten years old. I don't need you telling me what to do and what not to do. Speaking of telling kids what not to do, is Mia upstairs?"

"She left right after you did this morning," Monica said.

"She what?" I couldn't believe my ears. "She's grounded!"

Mom and Monica exchanged wide-eyed glances. "Guess she doesn't think so," Monica said.

Mom nodded. "Someone is going to be in really big trouble."

"Someone's already in really big trouble." I darted into the dining room to retrieve my handbag to excavate my cell phone. I checked the long, slender inside pocket where I'd determined I'd keep my phone. It wasn't there. If I had an ounce of self-discipline, maybe I could be an ounce organized.

I turned my bag over and dumped everything out onto the kitchen table.

"Cameron!" Mom said, shocked. "What a mess!"

"No time for a lecture, Mom." I grabbed my cell and dialed Ben's number. Once again, it went to voicemail. "Call me about your daughter. We have big problems with her."

"Well, that'll make him want to call back," Mom said.

I dropped my phone on the table and sank into a chair. "Did Mia say where she was going?"

"No." Monica folded the paper treat bags and fastened the tin ties. "Someone picked her up. I figured it was Steph."

"No, no, no," I said. "It's the boy. The *boy!*"

"What boy?" Mom and Monica asked in unison.

I told them what Soapy had told me.

"That can't be true," Mom said, placing both hands on the countertop like she felt faint. "Mia, staying out all night with a boy? No. I can't believe that."

"Soapy saw what he saw. I don't have her side of the story," I said.

"She's not a saint," Monica said. "She's not a bad kid, but she's a sixteen-year-old girl who isn't afraid to try things. She's going to push the boundaries, that's for sure."

"This is going beyond the boundaries." I tossed a chapstick and a pack of mints back in my handbag. "Ben's going to hit the roof."

"Do you have to tell him?" Monica asked.

"Of course I have to tell him."

"I was just thinking that maybe if you handled this and kept it between you and Mia, she'd appreciate it and not give you grief anymore."

"Plus you could hang it over her head," Mom said.

"I'm not blackmailing a teenager."

"When you have a strong-willed daughter, you use every tool in the shed." Mom quirked her eyebrows. "I should know."

"I never stayed out all night with a boy when I was in high school."

"Maybe I wasn't talking about you."

"Mom!" Monica shouted. "We were only friends. You know that. I fell asleep working on a Spanish project."

"So you say."

"Wouldn't I admit it by now?"

I put the last of my junk back in my purse and got up from the table. "I'm telling Ben. We're going to our Wednesday night movie tonight."

"Think about it," Monica said. "You'll win points with him if Mia respects your authority."

"I'll lose points if I don't tell him about this and he finds out. Half the town knows about it."

She just shrugged.

Maybe Monica had a point.

Mia and I had to come to an understanding somehow. Her disregard for my authority had to stop. She'd be terrified of her father finding out about what she'd done. His disapproval would devastate her. Maybe I could use this situation as a tool—a teaching tool, not a blackmailing tool. Between Mia and me, we could come to an understanding about her behavior and Ben wouldn't have to know about it. This must be how parenting worked.

I'd win this battle of wills. I felt like a veteran mom already.

· Fourteen ·

The twentieth jar of honey was capped when Mia came strolling home just after four o'clock in the afternoon. "Where have you been?" I asked.

"Steph's."

"I grounded you this morning."

"I had to work."

"We need to talk. Right now."

"Fine. Whatever."

Anna inhaled sharply. Her parents would probably throttle her if she spoke to them this way. "We'll put these jars in a box before we go," she said.

"Thank you, Anna."

Mia rolled her eyes.

"Upstairs," I said, grasping her wrist and pulling her inside. "This disrespect ends right now."

"It isn't disrespect. It's apathy."

I stopped mid-way up the stairs and spun around to face her. "Will you be apathetic when your father finds out you spent the night with a boy last night?"

Her face instantly turned white. "It wasn't like that. I swear!"

"I don't care what it was like." I continued up the stairs and into her room, closing the door behind us. "Did you think I wouldn't find out? You haven't lived in Metamora long, but I can assure you, you're lucky to go to the bathroom without everyone in town knowing about it."

"Eww."

"You get the point. Who is he?"

"Who is who?" she asked, dropping down on the end of her bed.

"The boy you were with last night—and today, I'm guessing."

"Does it matter?"

"You're digging your own grave here, Mia."

She huffed and bounced back to the head of her bed. "You know him, so I don't know why this is such a big deal. It's not what you think."

"I know him? Okay, then who is he?"

She pursed her lips and looked up at me under hooded eyelids. "Nick Valentine."

Nick Valentine? Nick had been one of my Action Agency members while working off his community service and being on probation for assault. He hung around with a bad crowd, wore rock band t-shirts, had spiked hair with bleached tips, and painted his nails black. Not to mention ... "He's like twenty years old! Good gravy! You're sixteen, Mia. You're in high school. He's got a criminal record!"

"You know he's not like that."

"Like what? Everything I just said is true."

"It's not like we were by ourselves. His boss, Avery Bantum, was with us. He owns a dog kennel and Nick works for him. It's not like he's a criminal. I know you don't think Nick's a bad guy." She picked up a stuffed bear and hugged it.

"I don't—I didn't—Mia, I don't know him well enough to say if he's okay for you to date. The point remains he's too old for you, regardless. He hangs around a bad crowd. His friend, Cory Bantum, Avery's brother I'm guessing, was killed last year. I don't want you around guys like Avery and Nick."

"It's not even—ugh! Why do you have to be like this? Why can't you trust my judgement?"

"Because you sneak around! How am I supposed to trust you?"

"So, what now?" Mia asked, tossing her bear aside. "You tell my dad and I get sent back to my mom in Columbus, right?"

"No."

"Yeah, right. Dad doesn't even live here and I'm causing you problems when you're already stressed, blah, blah, blah. I get it. I'll start packing my stuff."

"I said no, Mia. You're not going anywhere. You're going to be punished, but you're not getting shipped off."

"Oh." She folded her arms and sank back into her pillows. "Are you telling my dad?"

This was tricky. Was I going to tell Ben? I should, but I really wanted to handle the situation myself. I wanted to earn Mia's trust and respect. "I haven't decided."

She glanced up at me, hopeful. "I'll do anything—*anything*—if you don't tell him."

"The first thing you have to do is take your punishment like an adult. You got yourself into this mess, so you have to accept the consequences."

She took a deep breath, and nodded.

"No pageant," I said.

Her eyes widened. "What? You can't do that!"

"I can do that, and I am. Your punishment is that you can't participate in the pageant."

"That's not fair!"

"Not fair is breaking the rules and expecting nothing bad to happen."

"Grandma Irene won't stand for this."

"I guess if she doesn't she'll complain to your father, who will ask me why I'm not letting you participate. Then I'll have to tell him why. So, if I were you, I'd find a way to make sure Grandma Irene doesn't have a fit about it."

I felt terrible, but at the same time, this was working out better than expected. Irene couldn't come back on me about the punishment, either.

"I can't believe you would do this to me!" she yelled.

"It's your choice. Accept my punishment, or your dad can come up with one."

Mia threw herself face-first into her pillow, crying. "You're going to feel so bad for doing this!"

"It's not about me feeling good about punishing you. It's about you learning your lesson."

I left her room feeling light-headed. It was a confrontation I hadn't been looking forward to, but I think I'd done well. I held my ground and doled out her punishment. She'd think twice before seeing Nick Valentine again. At least without permission.

Downstairs, my Action Agency members had left. Mom, Quinn, and Monica were finishing up making the kitchen spotless, and the dogs were outside chasing each other around the backyard.

"Anna left the honey in the basement and that list on the fridge," Mom said, jutting her chin toward a paper stuck to the freezer door with a magnet.

It was a checklist of the items we had left to do for Canal Days. All of them were crossed off except one: getting the road that ran from Route 52 to the canal closed for vendor tables and pedestrians.

I'd talk to Ben about that when he picked me up in a couple of hours, and the last item on our long list would be completed. Even the fancy booths that Irene had demanded were checked off with a note stating that Old Dan's son, Frank, had called to say they were finished.

I felt a weight lift from my shoulders, like I'd been lugging Gus around all week and had just set him down.

"You look faint," Mom said, striding over to me and brushing my hair back from my forehead. "Are you feeling alright?"

"I think I'm in shock. We're actually going to pull this off. Canal Days is actually going to happen as planned." A giddy laugh escaped me.

"Both of my girls have succeeded!"

"You're finished with the treats?" I asked, Monica.

"One more kind to make tomorrow and I'll be finished." She wiped her hands on her flour-covered apron.

"What kind?" My house had smelled mouth-watering good all week. Savory Italian and then sweet like honey.

"Dogs Dig Leftovers!" She grinned and elbowed Quinn playfully.

"Nobody digs leftovers," he said.

There was obviously some joke between them about this last biscuit. "What's in it?"

"Pot roast, peas, and carrots."

"Seriously? I might take up a diet of dog treats." They sounded better than most of my meals.

"Just a small amount of lean beef minced with the vegetables and mixed with my biscuit dough," she said. "The grocery in Brookville has roasts on sale—buy one get one free. It inspired me."

My stomach growled. "You're making me hungry. I better call Ben and find out if we're going to dinner before the movie."

"You mean you're not going to make movie popcorn your dinner?" Mom asked, giving me the side-eye.

"I know. I know. You didn't raise me to live on junk food."

"I'm going to find a yoga class to sign you up for. You need something healthy in your life."

I stifled a groan. She was only here for a few more days, after all, and she meant well. But I did find it ironic that only minutes ago I was the one doling out the punishment, and now I was firmly under my own mom's thumb.

I wondered if it was karma or just bad luck.

∞

Ben snorted and coughed, trying not to choke on his soda. "Yoga?"

"I don't know why that's so funny," I said, glaring at the box of buttery popcorn on my lap. We were sitting in the middle of the center row of the theater, waiting for the movie to start.

"I've never known you to be … bendy."

"Bendy? What's that supposed to mean?"

"Yoga. Don't you have to stretch a whole bunch of different ways?"

"You don't think I can stretch different ways?"

"No, that's not what I mean. It just doesn't strike me as anything you'd actually want to do."

"Maybe I do. I don't know." Of course I didn't want to go to yoga, but I wasn't going to admit it to Ben. I didn't even want to admit it to myself. I needed an exercise regimen in my life, but didn't want to commit to going to a class once a week—or more. What if it was three times a week? I'd never make it. I didn't have the willpower or the self-discipline. That I *could* admit.

Ben patted my knee but knew better than to continue on the topic of yoga. "This movie's supposed to be good?"

"That's what Cass said." We were seeing something called *Sunset At Dawn*, and as far as I knew it was based on a book I'd never read or even heard of. Since there wasn't anything else playing we hadn't already seen in the past few weeks, Ben agreed to give it a shot.

The theater was practically empty, with only one other couple—in their early twenties by the looks of them—a few rows in front of us. That should've tipped me off.

The lights went down and the previews played through. I munched my popcorn and peanut M&M's. Then the opening scene flashed on-screen.

My mouth dropped open, releasing an M&M. It fell onto my lap and rolled to the floor.

Bodies. Dead, mutilated bodies filled the screen. It was horrific.

Then it got worse.

Zombies. Dead, decomposing zombies eating brains.

"What is this?" Ben whispered.

"I don't know."

"Cass said this was good?"

"Yes!"

The young girl in front of us looked over her shoulder "Shh!"

The monsters on screen were moaning, making an ungodly racket. One of them—the main character maybe?—caught sight of a dog and took chase after it.

"No!" I grabbed Ben's sleeve and hid my face in his shirt.

"It's okay," he said, stroking my hair. "That's one fast dog. He won't catch him."

I peeked at the screen just in time to see the dog slip into the woods and escape. "I don't think I can sit through this."

"I don't have any desire to sit through this," he said, laughing. "Cass…"

"Cass…" I shook my head, and started to laugh.

"Shh!" the girl in front of us shot back again.

"Come on." Ben took my hand and we left the theater.

Outside, we sat in the parking lot on the tailgate of his pickup, Metamora One. "That's the last time I take movie recommendations from Cass," I said, reaching for a handful of popcorn.

"You'd think having a boyfriend who makes documentaries she'd appreciate a different kind of movie than zombies. Don't get me wrong, a good zombie flick every now and then is okay, but that was over the top."

"That was gross."

"The dog did you in," he said, stealing my peanut M&M's.

"I can't help it. I live with too many of them."

"You're the leader of the pack."

"I try at least. I hear Avery Bantum took over the family kennel for his brother. I'm glad he kept it open." Cory Bantum had been a possible witness to the last murder in Metamora and ended up being the second victim. I'd spoken to him on the telephone once and only knew of him through passing comments from my neighbors, but he seemed to have a knack for finding trouble. Still, I was glad to know that his brother took on the dog kennel. He might be a good person for Monica to work with, giving samples to his boarders.

"I heard that, too. The guy's been arrested a few times, so I hope he's turned things around now that he's a business owner."

I thought of Mia hanging out with Nick and Avery. "Me, too. Hey, how's Brutus coming along with his training?"

"Good. Really good. Quinn has a gift, that's for sure. I never thought I'd see the day Brutus stayed on command."

"How long until he's an official K9 dog cop?"

"Let's not get ahead of ourselves. He's got a while."

"Does that mean Quinn's staying a long time?"

He eyed me shrewdly. "I see what you're asking. The answer is I have no idea. I'm not sure he even knows."

"What do you mean he doesn't even know?"

"I don't think he has any reason to go back home anytime soon."

"But maybe he has a reason to stay?"

"We can hope." He popped a couple peanut M&M's into his mouth. "What was going on with Mia today?"

A jolt of panic shot through me. "With Mia?"

"Cam, you left me two voicemails."

"Right. Well, um, it's nothing. I handled it. Just an argument."

"Didn't sound like nothing. Are you sure?"

I knew in my heart I should tell him, but I had handled it. He would kill me if he ever found out about Nick Valentine, but I couldn't betray Mia's trust. She and I had an understanding. I punished her and she was done seeing Nick. "I'm sure."

He sat up a little taller and smiled proudly.

"What?" I asked.

"You and Mia figuring things out. It makes me happy, Cam. I hope you know how much I love having her here, and how much—"

"I know," I said, not willing to hear what would come next. Guilt gnawed at me. He should be at home—at our home—with his daughter. Things were better now. He and I were better. And Mia was here. We could be a family.

"Things are good," he said, sensing my pangs of conscience. "Nothing needs to change."

"I know you can't live in Carl's gatehouse forever."

"But I can for now. He needs me, and Brutus and I are doing just fine there. I'm thinking of it as a work arrangement, not a marriage arrangement."

I wasn't sure if that was a good thing or a bad thing. If he wasn't facing the reason why we weren't living under the same roof, how could we make it better? I had to trust that our dating and getting to know one another again was working. It felt like it was.

Ben stuck his hand in his pocket and pulled out his cell phone, which was vibrating with a call. "Mom," he said. "If I don't answer, she'll call every ten minutes until I do."

"I know. Trust me. I know." The woman was a pest in a pantsuit.

"Hey, Mom," he said, putting the phone to his ear. "What are you talking about?" He glanced over at me. "Hold on. She's right here. Let me put you on speaker and you can ask her yourself."

No, I mouthed, but he did it anyway. "Okay, Mom, go ahead," he said.

"Cameron! Are you planning on selling my house right out from underneath me?" The screechiness of her voice surprised me. Any second her head might explode.

"Sell the house? No. Why would I—" Then it hit me. "Oh, Arnie Rutherford."

"Yes, Arnie Rutherford!" she shouted. "Elaina told Jim who told Stewart that you met with him today about selling the house!"

"He did say he has a client interested in making an offer, but that's not why I met with him, Irene. I'm not looking to sell Ellsworth House."

"Then why on earth would you have a meeting with him? He's a real estate tycoon, for Pete's sake."

"I had a few questions I wanted to ask him about, umm…" I glanced up at Ben, considering how I'd pacify Irene without tipping

145

him off that I was snooping into Butch's murder. "I needed to find out who to contact about the Landow Farm. To get the electric fence turned off for Canal Days."

Ben's eyes narrowed. He was no fool, and he knew me well.

"Oh," she said, calming a bit. "Well, okay then."

"Okay, Irene. I'm glad we had this chat. I'll let you talk to Ben again."

He took the call off of speaker and put the phone back to his ear. "Everything good now, Mom? Okay, then. Yeah, talk to you later."

I binged on the last few peanut M&M's while he said his goodbye and hung up. Lying and guilt made me an emotional eater.

"You know I'm not buying that story," he said, stuffing the phone back in his pocket.

"I do need the fence off, and Phillis Landow was being less than cooperative telling me if she was the one who could do it for me."

"And I'm sure he spilled the beans on the new owner of the farm."

"Actually, no, he didn't. He did warn me not to go digging for information, though."

He shook his head. "Which I'm sure you did anyway. Just like I'm sure last night you ran out of the Briar Bird for an Action Agency emergency that had nothing to do with Canal Days."

I shrugged, tired of lying. "Roy needed me to pick him up from the horse track. He was passed out cold when I got there."

"What was Roy doing at the horse track? Last I knew his only vice was whiskey, not betting the ponies."

"Well, the whiskey got him, and I shoveled him out of trouble. Literally."

He rolled his eyes, like Mia. "I don't want to know."

Let's keep it that way, I thought. The less Ben knew, the better off I would be, with Mia and with anything I discovered about Butch Landow's murder.

· Fifteen ·

Walking Gus and the twins was like leashing three giant Tasmanian devils and tugging them down the street.

My fur balls headed for the park. The grass was still wet with dew, and the sun wasn't showing its face from behind the dark, rolling clouds. It was gloomy even for an October morning.

Many of the homes along my path had jack-o-lanterns sitting out, carved and festive for Canal Days tomorrow. I spotted Spook winding his long, black tail around a pumpkin, his green eyes watching us pass by. This was his time of year.

Gus hurtled past the gazebo, Dumb and Dumber in his wake, and me bringing up the rear. "Gus, don't you dare!" I shouted, sensing he was headed for the canal. I'd been hauled in knee-deep more than a couple of times and didn't treasure the memories.

He looked back at me, brows cocked and doggy eyes innocent, as if to say, *Would I do that?*

"Come on, you three trouble makers." I tugged them toward the bridge over the canal, contemplating the thick, bristly coats of the twins. They needed grooming. When I got back to the house, I'd see if Monica

147

wanted to take a ride to Bantum Kennels to leave some Dog Diggity samples for Avery's customers, and while we were there I'd ask him if he knew of a good groomer.

The dogs loped over the bridge with me hanging on to their leashes for dear life.

"Morning!" Brenda Lefferts called from the doorway of her bookstore, Read and ReRead. She and I had become good friends over the past few years.

"Morning!" I called back, yanking the dogs toward her shop. "Ready for Canal Days?

"I'm putting out a table of gothic classics this year. *Dracula, Frankenstein, The Picture of Dorian Gray, The Strange Case of Dr. Jekyll and Mr. Hyde.* And tonight I'm inviting some friends in to get into the spirit of the season."

"The spirit of the season? Exhaustion and prayers for many, many sales?"

She laughed and adjusted the pins attaching the doily to the bun on the back of her head. "More like a Halloween party. I've always loved the costumes and pumpkins, the fantasy of dressing up and getting scared telling ghost stories. So you'll come tonight, right? I know it's last minute, but my cousin is driving in from Chicago and trust me, you won't want to miss meeting her."

"Of course I will. Sounds like fun."

"And bring Monica. And I hear your mom's in town."

"She is, but she's been spending most of her time with Carl Finch." I gave her a meaningful look.

"No!"

"Yes. They're thick as thieves, but I'll bring her along if she's home."

"And Monica has a new friend, too, I understand?"

"Quinn Kelly, the K9 trainer from Ireland. I wish he lived just a little closer."

"That is quite a distance. An ocean away."

"She'll be devastated when he leaves."

She frowned. "Maybe he'll stay, or ask her to go with him."

I didn't want to think of my sister moving to another country, another continent. "Maybe," I said, stroking Gus's soft, thick fur. He licked my hand, seeming to sense my distress. The twins started nipping at each other, playing. "I better get going. The natives are getting restless."

"Alright. I'll see you tonight. Seven o'clock."

The dogs and I said our goodbyes and continued on our way. A few doors down a big, black iron caldron sat in front of the Soapy Savant. Theresa was hauling a big box across the yard, and Soapy was tying cornstalks to their wrought iron fence with twine.

"What's your plan for the cauldron?" I asked. "Going to brew up a giant batch of coffee?"

"Not coffee," Soapy said. "Hot spiced apple cider."

Theresa plopped the box down beside the cauldron. "I've got dried oranges and cinnamon sticks, whole cloves, and allspice."

My mouth watered. "I can't wait to try it with one of Betty's snickerdoodles."

The snickerdoodles Betty sold in Grandma's Cookie Cutter were my favorite. She didn't always have them, so I stocked up when she made them.

I waved and went on my way, dogs in tow. Farther along the canal, between Cass's Fiddle Dee Doo Inn and Dog Diggity, a bandstand was being erected across from the gristmill. Frank Gardner, Will Atkins, and Old Dan were all busy sawing and hammering.

It seemed like the whole town was busy getting ready for tomorrow and the start of Canal Days. The preparations for our weekend festivities charged the air with excitement. Or maybe it was the storm brewing.

Thunder rumbled overhead, threatening to dampen our spirits. The wind blew, rattling the dried, dying leaves in the trees. My knee throbbed, the pulse reminding me that the sky would open up any minute. I hoped it would so the rain would end before tomorrow.

∞

I walked through the door of Ellsworth House to the smell of Sunday dinner on a Thursday morning. Monica was in the kitchen scooping dog biscuits off of a baking tray with her spatula. "How's it going?" I asked. "They smell incredible."

"A few more batches and I'll be ready for tomorrow."

Mom whisked in from the patio holding Liam. "What a good little boy you are," she told him, using baby-talk. "You're the cutest little thing in the whole wide world." The big dogs scampered in circles around her. "Not you!" she shouted at them. "You're hairy beasts!" She sat Liam on the floor and patted each of the beastly dogs on the head. "Rotten mongrels."

"What do you two have planned for tonight?" I asked them.

"Am I supposed to have plans?" Mom asked.

"You've had plans every night since you got here."

"Well, not tonight," she said.

"How about you, Mon?" I asked, scooting in beside her to wash my hands at the kitchen sink.

"I'm free until around eight. Quinn's training Brutus after Ben gets off work, then we're getting together."

"Great, you're both coming with me to Read and ReRead. Brenda's having a Halloween party."

"A Halloween party?" Mom said, pouring a cup of coffee. "I haven't been to one of those since I was in my twenties."

"From what I gather this is just a small get-together to kick off the festivities and to welcome Brenda's sister to town and introduce her to a few friends."

"Do we need costumes?" Mom asked. She couldn't hide the glimmer in her eyes even if she tried. Mom always had a flare for the dramatic. Costumes were right up her ally.

"I'm not wearing a costume," Monica was quick to add.

"Party pooper. Cam will wear one with me, won't you?"

Brenda *had* mentioned costumes. "Why not? Sounds fun."

The last time I'd worn a costume was over the summer to a Civil War reenactors' dinner. I ended up on my hoop-skirted bottom on the floor of the Briar Bird dining room among shards of my broken dinner plate. Not my finest hour. This time I'd stick with something easy. No hoop skirts.

"Monica, when you're done baking, let's drive up the road to Connersville. Cory Bantum's brother, Avery, took over the kennel. You can leave some samples for his customers, and I need to find out if there's a good groomer to take Jekyll and Hyde to.

"Jekyll and Hyde!" Monica trilled. "Those are perfect names for them!"

I pondered the idea for a minute. Gus, Isobel, Liam, Jekyll, and Hyde. I wasn't sure the names fit with my brood. It did fit with their personalities though. Crazy and scary. "I'll think about it."

"Give me about fifteen minutes and I'll be ready to go with you," she said.

"Want to ride along with us, Mom?" I asked, grabbing a wicker basket out of the pantry for Monica's samples.

"Sure, why not? I am here to visit you girls, after all. By the way, did Elaina leave any yarn in Dog Diggity after her shop moved out?"

"There's still a bunch in a cupboard unless Johnna got her paws on it. Why, what are you thinking?" I doubted it would be anything easy, like some green face paint and a broom to go as witches.

"Oh, you'll see. Let's stop by the store so I can get some of that yarn. All I need from you is a sweatshirt you can wear. I'll do the rest."

"Sounds ominous," Monica said.

I nodded in agreement. This would prove interesting—and most likely embarrassing.

The front door squeaked open. "Morning! Anybody home?" Ben called.

"In here," I said, hearing his footsteps already making their way down the hall toward us.

"Look at these three lovely ladies," he said. "Where's Mia?"

"Sleeping. She hasn't been down yet."

An icy fear crept over me. I hadn't peeked in her bedroom this morning. What if she defied me and spent another night in the company of Nick Valentine? No. She wouldn't do that. Would she?

"I'll go see if she's awake," I said, darting past him and dashing up the stairs as quickly as my knee would let me.

Mia's door was closed. I knocked. "Mia? Your dad's here."

No answer.

I knocked again, a little harder. "Mia?"

After a few more seconds with no reply, I turned the knob and cracked the door open.

There she lay, sound asleep with headphones over her ears. I crept in and sat on the side of her bed. "Mia," I said, easing the headphones off of her ears, "your dad's downstairs."

She grunted and rolled over, so I shook her shoulder. "Hey, it's time to get up. Come on down and tell your dad good morning."

Her eyes shot open. "He's home? Did he move back home?"

It was early, not as early as she might have thought since she slept like every other teenager on the planet—late and like the dead. Seeing her so excited about having her dad down in the kitchen when she woke up made me feel like an actual wicked witch. "No, honey, he didn't move back in. He just stopped by this morning before work."

"Oh." She threw back her covers and swung her feet to the floor. Disappointment was written all over her face.

"I'll go let him know you're coming down, okay?"

She nodded and rubbed her eyes. At times like this, when she was sleepy and her hair was tousled, she still looked like the little girl I'd met five years ago.

I left her bedroom, closing the door behind me, and made my way back down the stairs. At the bottom, the door off the hallway leading down to the basement was open. Ben stood two steps down looking into the darkness, breathing hard.

"Why are you thinking about going down there?" I asked.

"I ran into Roy at Soapy's. He said there are a couple boxes of jarred honey in the basement that you're planning to sell for the Action Agency to buy new desks. I figured I'd run them over to Dog Diggity for you along with Monica's biscuits."

"What a guy!" Mom shouted from her seat at the kitchen table.

I leaned in closer to Ben so she wouldn't hear me. "You don't have to do this." Ben had a fear of dark basements. It was the one thing my tough policeman husband had a hard time facing. Not bad guys with guns, but damp, musty, dim basements. I'd never gotten to the bottom of why he had his fear. I figured it must have had something to do with believing in monsters when he was a young kid. Or maybe he accidentally got locked in down there or something. I had to admit, Ellsworth House's basement, without electric light fixtures, was creepy. There was a root cellar with a hard dirt floor that I found a bit too dungeon-like for my comfort.

I was just glad the laundry hook-ups had been moved to a big closet off of the dining room so I didn't have to go down there practically at all.

Ben took another step down, flicking on his flashlight. The beam shook and wavered. "I'll be right back up," he said, more for his own benefit than mine.

"I'll come with you."

The wooden stairs were ancient and the whole case seemed to wobble slightly with each footstep. Whether they actually moved or it was just my imagination, I wasn't sure.

In front of me, Ben moved as slowly as a turtle.

An arthritic turtle.

I fought the urge to grab the flashlight and run down the stairs past him. I took a few steps more and went face first into a sticky spiderweb. It clung to my forehead. I swiped it off, not able to get all of it, and felt something crawling in my hair. A spider!

I screamed. Ben screamed. He hurled himself around and grabbed me around my waist. We both went toppling down the last few stairs, like Jack and Jill, to the gritty basement floor below. The dogs, barking at the top of their lungs, came bounding down the steps. The flashlight cracked against the cement and went out, leaving us in pitch blackness.

"Ouch," Ben said, untangling his long legs from mine, and shoving Gus out of his face.

"Cameron? Ben?" Mom called from the basement door. "What's going on down there?"

"It was only a spider," I called back, pushing one of the twin tanks away. "We're okay."

"Well, I didn't think it was the boogey man! Good gracious! All that screaming! Give a woman a heart attack, why don't you?"

The dogs quickly lost interest in us and started sniffing around the basement. Ben got to his feet and gripped my hand, helping me up. "Sorry," he mumbled, obviously ashamed.

"Well, that was the quick way down. Let's get the honey and go back up."

Up in the hall, Monica called the dogs, luring them back to the kitchen with promises of treats. They bounded up the steps, leaping over one another to be the first to the top.

Ben scrounged around for the flashlight. He picked it up and shook it, then knocked it against the heel of his hand a few times. Finally, it flickered back to life. He scanned the basement. A pair of glowing green-yellow eyes caught in the beam. Ben gasped. "Darn cat," he said.

"Good gravy, Spook! How did you get down here?"

The cat went skittering past us with a mouse in his mouth and up the stairs."

"Pandemonium is about to break out," Ben said.

"I don't think so. It's like he's invisible to the dogs. I don't know how he does it."

"Maybe he really is some kind of phantom cat."

"I wouldn't put it past him," I said, spotting the boxes of honey sitting on top of a couple old milk crates against the wall. "There they are."

We each hefted one into our arms and headed back upstairs. "That was too adventurous for this early in the morning," Ben said, once we were back in the hallway. He lowered his box so I could set mine on top. I took the flashlight out of his hand and opened the front door for him, following him out to Metamora One to stash the boxes in the pickup bed.

"What's with the duck?" he asked, eyeing Metamora Mike sunning himself in Old Dan's lawn chair beside the bee box.

"He thinks he a dog. He's joined the pack."

"You're running a zoo here, Cam."

Didn't I know it.

"Daddy!" Mia ran across the yard and into Ben's arms.

"Morning, beautiful," he said, kissing the top of her head. "I have time to grab breakfast before work, want to come with me?"

She'd already gotten dressed and pulled her hair up into a pony tail. "Can we get pancakes?"

"Of course. Let me grab Monica's biscuits and we'll go. Cam, want to come?"

"I think I'll let you guys have some father-daughter time. I've got a million things to do today anyway."

"Call if you need me to help with anything," he said.

Over the past few years Ben had been too busy with work to worry about what I was doing, or if I needed help with anything. It seemed he had turned over a new leaf after all.

"I will." A warmth overtook me, and I reached up on tip-toe to kiss his cheek. "Thanks."

He smiled and gave me a wink. "That's what husbands are for, right?"

Every day we were separated brought us one step closer together.

Odd how that happened.

I was just glad it did.

· Sixteen ·

$\mathcal{O}$n the backseat of Monica's car, Mom was making pom-pons out of brown yarn. If this was going to be my costume, I didn't want to think about what it was turning into. Something with spots perhaps? A giraffe or a cheetah? Grandma Diggity?

Connersville wasn't far, only one town away. The Whitewater Valley train came and went from Connersville to Metamora a few times each day. In the next couple of days, it would bring in tourists, and the conductor, Roger Tillerman, would be dressed as a vampire, like every other year during Canal Days.

"Mon, up here next to the Kroger is McDonald's, see it?" I pointed up ahead. "I need a cheeseburger. I'm having withdrawal symptoms."

"Like what?" Mom said from the backseat. "Did you lose a pound or two from not eating fast food?"

I scowled out the window and waited for another yoga comment. McDonald's cheeseburgers were one of my vices. Cookies and cheeseburgers, so sue me. I didn't drink like Roy, or gamble like the recently departed Butch. Food was my weakness.

Monica turned in and cruised into the drive through lane. "Mom, do you want anything?" she asked.

Reluctantly, Mom ordered a yogurt parfait and an iced tea, while Monica and I got burgers and fries. We took after Dad—and most of America—in our love of unhealthy eating. Mom was on her own with her yogurt. Well, she always had Mia, I guess. They could console one another over the lack of vegetables in my refrigerator's vegetable drawer.

We scarfed down our lunch as Monica drove and had just finished when she pulled into the parking lot of Bantum Kennels. We were the only car there. It was eerily familiar. The last time I'd been here, the place had been ransacked and Cory Bantum lay shot out back by the dog runs.

"Slow day, I guess," Monica said, turning off the car's engine.

"I'll stay here while you two run in," Mom said, consumed with her yarn project.

"We won't be long." I got out of the car and waited for Monica to collect the basket of samples from her trunk.

The sky over Connersville was dark and cloudy, too. "If this rain doesn't break or pass over us, I'm afraid it'll hit tomorrow," I said. "That's the last thing we need after all the hard work we've done."

Monica patted my arm. "The vendors will bring tents to put their tables under, and everyone else will have an umbrella. Don't worry."

"Yeah, you're right. I'm sure it'll be fine."

But my knee begged to differ as pain shot through it on the way to the kennel entrance. This storm would be a doozie.

We walked inside to absolute silence. Nobody sat behind the front desk. The place was a ghost town.

"Why aren't there dogs barking?" Monica asked. "Have you ever been to a kennel and not heard dogs barking?"

"No." I searched the desk for a bell to ring for service, but there wasn't one. Oddly enough, there was a computer with a security monitor showing the parking lot on screen. I could make out Mom sitting in the back of Monica's car.

"Hello?" Monica called. "Anyone here?" She headed behind the desk toward the swinging double doors leading to the kennels.

Curious about the security cameras and sensing that something wasn't what it seemed, I sneaked around to the other side of the desk for a look at a few printed documents lying beside a keyboard. The first was a receipt from the kennel to a boarder for seven days, $420. Good gravy, that was a lot of money.

I shifted the receipt aside. Underneath was a certificate of deposit to an account in the kennel's name to Connersville First Bank for over three thousand dollars. I picked up the copy of the boarder's receipt again, and my blood froze. The $420 paid to the kennel was from Stewart Hayman. My in-laws didn't even own a dog.

"There's nobody back there," Monica said, coming back through the swinging doors. "And not one dog."

"Something's going on here," I said. "Something—" My eye caught on the corner of a bank receipt sticking out of the top drawer of the desk. The account was for Track Times, Inc. I reached for it.

"Can I help you?" a man asked, pushing through the doors behind Monica.

I dropped my hand, clasping it with my other in front of me.

"There you are," Monica said. "Avery?"

The tall, light-haired man who looked to be in his early forties glanced between us. "Yes. Who are you?"

He wasn't exactly friendly for a business owner, but the fishy pieces of this mystery were swimming laps in my head and almost fitting together.

"I'm Monica Cripps, and this is my sister, Cameron—"

"Cripps-Hayman," he said. "You found my brother's killer."

"I'm sorry for your loss," I said. "I'm glad you were able to keep the kennel open."

His eyes widened. "Right. It's been hard. Not a lot of business since Cory was found in the back. Some months I'm not making ends meet, unfortunately."

Monica thrust the basket of samples into his hands. "I make dog treats. I thought your customers might like some free samples for their pets."

"Oh. Okay. I'll set them here on the desk."

"Great! Cameron, didn't you have something to ask Mr. Bantum?"

My mind hit a wall. Didn't I have something to ask him? I had several questions to ask him, like why was there a bank receipt with Track Times written on it? Track Times, which now owned Butch Landow's farm. How could he afford a deposit of three thousand dollars and not be able to make ends meet?

"Cam?" Monica said, eyeing me warily. "Grooming?"

"Oh! Right! Do you happen to know of a good groomer? I'm on the hunt for one."

"No, I don't."

He was very direct, almost alarmingly so. "Too bad," I said. "Guess we'll get going."

I shot Monica a look that said, *Let's get the heck out of here,* turned for the door, and came face-to-face with Nick Valentine. "Nick!"

"Cameron. Hi. Haven't seen you for a while." His eyes shifted nervously between Avery and I.

"Not since you finished your community service hours," I said. I didn't know if he was nervous because I'd found out about him and Mia, or if it had something to do with Avery. "How've you been?"

"Good. I'm working here a few hours a week. Keeping busy."

"Good. Staying out of trouble then?"

He smiled, but it didn't reach his eyes. "Trying to."

"Well, it was good seeing you," I said. "Monica and I were just leaving."

"Hi, Nick," she said, on her way past and out the door. "Bye, Nick." She laughed and jogged to catch up with me, her feet crunching on the gravel behind me. "What's going on with you?" she asked when we got to her car.

"Get in. There's a camera on us."

"A camera?"

"Get in the car, Monica." We both hurried into our seats, yanking the car doors shut behind us. "Hurry up and get out of here," I said.

She threw the car in reverse and gunned the engine, throwing rocks.

"Not that fast, Luke Duke! Good gravy, let's not give it away that we know anything."

"I don't know anything!" she said. "You told me to hurry, so I'm hurrying."

Back out on the road, I breathed a little easier.

"What on earth is going on?" Mom said, picking up yarn pom-pons that had rolled to the floor when Monica peeled out of the parking lot.

"That kennel's not a kennel," I said.

"What are you talking about?" Monica said. "It looked like a kennel to me."

"There were no dogs. Don't you find that odd?"

"He said he'd been having trouble with business."

"He had a bank deposit slip on the desk for three grand. If he's doing three grand worth of business, he should have at least one dog in there, shouldn't he?"

"Slow week?"

"What about the receipt sticking out of the desk with Track Times written on it?"

"Track Times?"

I couldn't keep straight who I'd told what information to, the Action Agency or Mom and Monica. "Butch Landow's farm went to a company called Track Times."

"Money laundering," Mom said, half paying attention in the back seat. "Oldest trick in the book."

"What do you mean?" I asked, swiveling around to face her.

"I mean the kennel is a front for a dirty business, probably whatever Track Times is. That's why there weren't any dogs in there. It's the legal entity used to keep money in the bank so it doesn't look suspicious."

"Good gravy. What has Stewart gotten himself involved in."

"What about Stewart?" Mom asked.

"He paid the kennel over four hundred dollars to board a dog."

"I didn't know Irene and Stewart had a dog."

"They don't," Monica said. "Irene hates dogs."

"Oh," Mom said, "right. He's involved in this somehow." She made a *tsk tsk* sound with her tongue. "How are you going to break it to Ben?"

"I have no idea."

Ben would be devastated to find out his father was involved in illegal activity, and I would be devastated telling him.

∞

I woke up later that afternoon after giving in to a raging headache, taking two Tylenol, and collapsing in bed for a nap. The house was quiet for a change. Traipsing downstairs, the dogs were in the family room, snoozing in front of a fire in the fireplace. Mia was curled up in a chair texting, with Liam and a soft blanket over them. Mom and Monica were sipping hot tea and working a puzzle on the coffee table. It was a picture of tranquility.

"Every day needs to be like this," I said, pouring myself a cup of tea from the heavy cast iron tea pot sitting on its warmer before plopping down on the couch. It was a nice respite from the busy days leading up to tomorrow's Canal Days kick off.

"Your costume for tonight is on the kitchen table," Mom said, fitting a piece of the puzzle.

Before I got too comfortable, I got up and went in the kitchen to take a look. I held up my now totally unfamiliar sweatshirt in front of me. "What on earth is this?" It had the brown yarn pom-pons sewn all over the front and back with long pieces of off-white and red yarn hanging from everywhere else.

"Spaghetti and meatballs!" Mom said, clapping her hands together. "Isn't it clever? You wear a strainer on your head!"

"No," I said. "I'm not leaving the house as spaghetti and meatballs."

"Come on, Cam," she said. "I saw it a few years ago in a *Family Circle* magazine and always wanted to try it out."

"Then *you* wear it. I'm not five years old anymore, Mom."

"Well, I'm most definitely too old to wear it. It'll be perfect for you. You have that kind of personality."

"What kind is that?"

"Random," Monica said, while at the same time, Mom said, "Whimsical."

"Huh. I think you both have it out for me."

"Grandma Irene canceled the pageant," Mia said.

"Why?" I tossed the yarn-covered sweatshirt aside and gave all of my attention to my stepdaughter.

"Because I'm not going to be in it."

"Did you tell her *why* you aren't going to be in it?"

"I told her I didn't want to."

"So she canceled it? Because you don't want to be in it?"

"Why else would she be having it at all? Do you think she cares about any other girl winning?"

"No, not even a little bit."

I hadn't wanted the pageant to begin with, but now that it was canceled last minute I wondered how many girls and their parents were put out after buying dresses and shoes. And how many of them would blame me? I had to do something for them.

Jekyll, or maybe it was Hyde, it was hard to tell them apart, came up to me with my spaghetti and meatballs sweatshirt over his head. "You want to wear it?" That's when it struck me like lightning. A pet parade. The Metamora teens and their pets! The girls could still wear their dresses and parade their costumed pets along the canal. "Here," I told my bristly-furred friend, "let me help you." I lifted each paw into a sleeve and tugged the shirt over his head. It was a little big, but it worked. "Hey Mom, how fast can you make a couple more of these?"

"What on earth for?"

"A Canal Days Pet Parade!"

"When did you plan this?" Monica asked.

"Just now. Mia, ask your grandmother to get me the list of girls who were planning on being in the pageant, please."

"Why, so they can dress up like dogs and parade around?"

"No, of course not. Please just get me the list."

"Okay, whatever you say." She rolled her eyes and began texting again.

Mom got a bag of yarn from the hall closet and set it on the couch. "Well, let's start making meatballs, girls."

∞

We worked until six o'clock, only taking a break to make sandwiches for a quick dinner. Mia pitched in, giving up some of her old shirts

164

for the dogs' costumes. For Liam, we used one of Ben's old sweat socks and cut off the toe.

Instead of using strainers on their heads, we made elastic head-bands with one giant yarn meatball that would sit right between their ears. Liam's tube sock made him look more like a slice of lasagna than spaghetti and meatballs, but he fit right in with the rest of them.

"Now what are the three of us going to wear to Brenda's party?" Mom asked.

"I'm not dressing up," Monica said.

"Oh yes, you are. Don't be a party pooper." Mom tugged playfully on a lock of her hair.

"Mom, we have to be there in an hour," I reminded her. "There's not enough time."

"I know what to do," Mia said. "Get dressed in normal clothes, and I'll get your 'costumes' ready."

I was afraid to ask. I think Mom and Monica were, too, so we did what we were told and hightailed it upstairs to change for the party.

As I dressed in jeans and a sweater, I started worrying about Stewart and what he'd gotten himself tangled up in with Avery Bantum. How was he involved in Track Times and what Mom believed was a money-laundering scheme? And what did it have to do with Butch Landow? Could it be tied to his murder somehow?

The phone rang, breaking my string of mental questions. "Hello?" I answered, picking up the ancient rotary phone on my nightstand.

"He's out!" Cass screamed. "Andy's out of jail!"

"What? Cass, are you serious?"

"She's serious," Andy's voice said. I could hear Cass having fits of happiness in the background. "All I know is that there's new evidence and they let me and John and Paul go."

"That's fantastic! It's so good to hear from you! Are you doing okay? Do you need anything?"

"Just to get behind my camera again. Cass told me Old Dan's been helping you out over there."

"Did she tell you about the beehive?"

"In the porch column?"

"It's not in the porch column anymore. He built a bee box and moved them in. We have honey for days."

"Wow, the old man showed me up. I've been battling those bees for months."

"Well, now you can find a way to get Metamora Mike out of my yard. He's a dog treat addict."

"How did that happen?"

"Long story involving a clarinet and a model train."

"I don't want to know," he said, laughing.

"I guess this means we won't be seeing Cass at Brenda's party tonight."

"No way. I'm not letting her out of my sight."

"Thanks for calling and letting me know you're a free man again. Have a good night, Andy."

We said goodbye and hung up. I was more than relieved to hear that he and John and Paul were out of jail, but I was also concerned about what new evidence the police found. Maybe I should call Ben? My stomach clenched with the thought. If I had him on the phone, I'd have no reason to keep what I knew about Stewart from him. If I didn't talk to him, I could keep thinking about the best way to break the news.

For now, while there was still a killer on the loose, at least my friends were all in the clear of being convicted.

"Are you ready?" Monica asked, knocking on my door.

"I'm ready." I opened it and told her the good news.

"Thank goodness. I can't imagine how they kept them for as many days as they did."

We went downstairs to find Mom with a pair of scissors hanging around her neck by twine. "What's this?" I asked.

Mia picked up another twine necklace from the table, this one with a rock tied to it, and hung it around my neck. Then she hung a third with a sheet of paper dangling from it, around Monica's neck. "Paper, rock, scissors," she said. "Your costumes."

"How adorable!" Mom said, hugging Mia. "You're as smart as you are pretty."

"Great idea, Mia," Monica said, giving the next hug.

"Thanks," I said to her. "It really is a great costume for three people. What made you think of it?"

She shrugged. "It just came to me."

"Are you going anywhere tonight?"

"I'm grounded, remember?"

"Right answer," I said. "Just testing you. We won't be long."

"Be as long as you want. Doesn't matter to me. I'll be here wasting my life either way."

"Sounds like a good time to study."

She rolled her eyes. Someday they would get stuck like that, if my grandma knew what she was talking about. I'd been told that enough times when Mia was my age. I never believed it, but now that I was on the receiving end, I kind of hoped it was true.

"Come on, Rock," Mom said from the front door. "Time to rock and roll." She burst out laughing.

"Cut it out, Scissors," I said.

"This is going to be the longest hour of my life," Monica said, shaking her head.

Mom was already outside. "What are you waiting for, Mon, your walking papers?" She howled with laughter, making the dogs run to the windows barking.

We walked down the road and over the bridge in the waning moonlight filtering between the thick black clouds. The wind had kicked up and blew ripples across the canal. Mike and his harem of lady ducks quacked and flew into the empty horse stalls where the draft horses that draw the canal boat from the banks rest during their working hours. The leaves on the trees were showing their silver sides, which meant it was going to rain soon. I'd learned that from John Bridgemaker.

The palpable static in the air from the looming storm mixed with what I was keeping from Ben about his father, and the worry over tomorrow's festivities being rained out, had me on edge.

Something was about to break, I just wasn't sure what or how to prepare for it.

· Seventeen ·

*E*laina had a clock on a thick chain around her neck and a baseball hat on backwards. "I'm Grandma Diggity, you dig?" she folded her arms over her chest in a rapper pose. It was quite the costume for a ninety-three-year-old woman.

"Rock, paper, scissors!" Brenda said. "What a great idea!"

She ushered us in to the back where she kept an area clear for author visits and book signings. She'd decorated a table with handmade black paper flowers in vases and miniature pumpkins. The centerpiece was a tall owl statue painted black and silver. It reminded me of the antique owl fireplace andirons that used to be at Ellsworth House—before Irene stole and sold them and one ended up a murder weapon.

A chill slid down my back and I turned away from the decoration.

"Cameron," Brenda said, leading a stout, older woman in a purpled and silver headscarf up to me. "This is my cousin, Amelia."

"Nice to meet you, Amelia," I said, shaking her hand.

Amelia turned my hand over and regarded my palm. "Interesting," she said. "You've experienced a lot of change in the recent past."

It wasn't a question, she was reading my palm. "You're always in the midst of things. In the midst of tragedy and trouble, but you're a savior, too—you save people from trouble and harm. Are you a police officer?"

"No, but my husband is."

She looked closer at my palm. "Your husband. I see."

Did she see me having a husband? If so, was it for much longer? I was afraid to ask.

"Did you get something to drink, Cam?" Brenda asked. "There's punch on the table."

"Thanks, I'll get some." I wouldn't. I wasn't going anywhere near that owl. I eased my hand out of Amelia's, put it on Monica's back, and eased her over in front of me. "Amelia, this is my sister, Monica."

Monica shook hands and had hers confiscated. "I see you have new love in your life," Amelia said. "And he's Irish isn't he? Well, you're going to love our little treat we have planned, isn't she, Bren?"

I walked away before I could hear any more, like about how Monica was destined to move to Ireland.

Palm reading wasn't real. Certainly Brenda filled her cousin in on all of us and dressed her up in her headscarf to play the part for the party. I wondered if the punch was spiked. I could use a little nip of something to help calm my rattled nerves and enjoy the festivities.

I made my way to the other side of the table where Sue was chatting with Betty. Sue was dressed as an old-fashioned soda jerk, a costume she broke out every Canal Days for her Soda Pop Shop. Betty wore a blue, fuzzy sweater with googly eyes on the front. "Are you Cookie Monster?" I asked.

"Of course I am. Did you see the cookies I brought?" She pointed to a tray of round sugar cookies iced with blue squiggly fur, complete with big googly eyes like her sweater and a mini chocolate chip cookie sticking out where the mouth should be.

"Those are so cute, Betty," I said. "Are you selling those at your table tomorrow?"

"Those and a whole slew of other monster cookies. That's my theme this year. But don't worry, I made snickerdoodles, too, just for you."

"You're too good to me," I said, giving her shoulders a squeeze. "Cass called me and told me Andy's home."

"I heard. That poor boy should've never been arrested to begin with."

"They must know who really did it if they let all of them go," Sue said. "I hope they arrest someone soon." She rubbed her arms. I noticed she had goose bumps.

Thunder cracked, echoing through the old building.

"I think it's time," Amelia called out, smiling mysteriously.

"Everyone please follow me upstairs," Brenda said.

The door in the very back left corner of the bookstore opened to a stairwell leading up to Brenda's apartment on the second and third floors.

Judy came rushing in just in time, lowering her umbrella. "It's starting to come down out there," she said. "Sorry I'm late."

"You're just in time," Brenda said, stashing Judy's umbrella in a stand by the door.

"Wonder what's in store for us upstairs," Theresa whispered in my ear, coming up behind me. "A seance, perhaps?"

"I hope not. The last thing I need is a rogue spirit following me home. I already have a cat who wanders in uninvited and a duck that's surprisingly loud."

Theresa let out a sharp laugh. "Out of everyone here you would definitely be the one to attract a stray ghost."

"She's a stray magnet," Johnna said, reaching between us for a Cookie Monster cookie. "And a dead person magnet."

I couldn't argue her on either point.

We all trodded up the steps single file into Brenda's spacious living room lit with nothing but about a hundred candles. The shades were drawn, but a steady patter hit the window panes behind them. A room divider was set up in the corner, behind it more candles flickered. The building creaked as a gust of wind howled through the floor above us.

"Amelia is a fortune teller by trade," Brenda said. "I don't personally partake in the activities she specializes in, but I recognize the fun in it for a Halloween party. She's going to set up behind the divider and one at a time, you can go have your fortunes told. Then when you come out the rest of us can pester you for the details." She laughed.

"I'll go first," Monica said, darting forward. She saw me looking at her, questioning her eagerness. "What? I have to leave early."

She disappeared with Amelia behind the divider. Mom sneaked closer, hoping to catch a snippet of their conversation, I was certain.

"Are you going to do it?" Sue asked, jutting her chin toward the closed off area.

"I don't know. Are you?"

"I don't know. I kind of like having life be a surprise, especially the bad parts."

I nodded, knowing what she meant. The last thing Sue needed after losing her oldest daughter over the summer was any bad news. "I'm sure Brenda told her what to say to each of us," I said.

"True. I don't believe in hocus pocus like this, do you?"

"No." But it still creeped me out.

Brenda passed around glasses of warm mulled wine, which eased my nerves a bit. Elaina downed a glass and was trying to rap "Blue Suede Shoes" while winding the oversized alarm clock to the beat.

Theresa yawned. "I would've felt terrible for not coming tonight, but after all the Canal Days prep, I'm exhausted. I spent the afternoon making fancy pumpkin-shaped guest soaps. I'm going to have to leave soon and get to bed if I'm going to be worth anything tomorrow."

I needed to get home soon myself, and make a bunch of calls to invite the town teens and tweens to bring their pets to the parade.

Thunder rumbled overhead again, and lightning flashed beyond the window shades.

I really hoped there would be a parade.

Monica emerged from behind the divider glowing. Whatever Amelia told her had her floating on air. "She asked for you next, Cam," she said.

"I'm not sure—"

"Go!" Mom said. "Have some fun!"

I sat my mostly empty glass of wine down and stepped behind the divider. Taking that step was like walking off a tight rope without knowing if there was a net below. I reminded myself that whatever Amelia said, it was planted by Brenda. This was only a party game.

"Take a seat," Amelia said, smiling. "We can do this a couple of ways. I can continue reading your palm, or we can read cards, or tea leaves."

I wasn't thirsty, so tea leaves were out, and I'd had enough of her holding my hand. "Cards," I said.

She picked up a deck of large painted cards. Tarot cards, I figured, although I'd never seen any in real life, only on TV. She had me select a few, but not look at them, then she laid them out in a cross pattern. "Alright, let's begin."

She flipped the first and narrowed her eyes. Then she flipped the second, and made a humming noise. After the third, she said, "I see." She continued on like that until they were all face up. "Well there's a lot here," she said. "There's a bit of marital strife, but it's passing. Something ongoing with in-laws, something particularly troubling about your father-in-law. Then there's a daughter, or stepdaughter I think since there's this other woman in the dark over here," she tapped one of the cards. "Nothing more than normal teen and mother angst. Nothing to worry over there." She set two fingers on a pair of cards. "Your family ties are growing or strengthening. Both perhaps. Marriages, adoptions..." She wobbled her head back and forth. "It's growing and will continue to for some time. This one though," she said, jabbing a finger to the card in the dead center, "is disturbing. There's someone in need of help. Your help. He's in a barn and needs rescuing. Does that mean anything to you?"

Someone in a barn who needs saving? "Oh, Roy. That already happened."

"No, it's still here in the cards."

Well cards or not, it happened. "I think I know what it means."

"You can help this person?" She shook her head. "Maybe not a person, I see an animal."

A horse, or several, at the race track in the barn with Roy. "That makes sense. I've got it covered."

"Good," she said, sitting back. "Then there's only the father-in-law, but that's removed from your immediate influence, although it could come around into your house, so to speak."

"My house?"

"Planetary house. I read the stars as well."

"I see."

"So all good things, just watch out for anyone in need of rescuing in a barn."

"Will do. Thanks, Amelia."

"You're welcome. Can you send Elaina back please?"

"Elaina? Sure. Good luck."

She laughed. "You'd be surprised what that woman's palm has to say."

"I'm sure it has something to do with polka dots." Amelia gave me a confused look. "I'll send her back," I said, and stepped out from around the divider.

I sent Elaina back to have her fortune told. I wan't surprised by Amelia knowing about Roy in the barn. If Johnna new about it, the whole town did, so Brenda would've let her in on that tidbit. But Stewart was a whole different kettle of fish. Nobody other than Mom and Monica knew about Stewart and what we'd found at the kennel.

Maybe there was a little merit to this fortune reading stuff after all.

∞

When the fortune telling was over and everyone was back downstairs, Betty brought out a large round loaf of bread stuffed with raisins. "Barmbrack is a customary Irish Halloween tradition," she said. "It just so happens that this year we have an Irish visitor to our town, which reminded me of this. Each of you will get a slice. Inside there will be a token. Depending on which you get, it will be your fortune for the coming year."

Betty sliced the loaf and sat the raisin bread on plates for us to select our own. "Now be careful and don't choke on the tokens inside," she said.

We all dug in. The first to find one was Sue. "I think it's a pea," she said.

"The pea means you won't be getting married in the next year," Betty said. "Sorry, dear."

We all laughed. Sue wasn't dating anyone at the moment. She'd had her eyes set on Carl for the longest time, but he'd never returned the affection and now Mom was in the picture, at least for a couple more days.

"I'll survive," Sue said.

"I found something," Monica said, digging it out with her fork. "It's a ring."

"That means you'll be wed within a year," Betty said.

Mom clasped her hands together. Monica beamed. I wondered how that could be with a man who lived so far away.

Elaina's alarm clock around her neck sounded. It was eight o'clock. "Oh, I've got to run," Monica said. She bounded over and gave Brenda a big hug, and then Amelia. "This was a great party. Thanks so much for inviting me."

"I'm going, too," I said. "Mom, are you going to stay a while, or come with us?"

"I think I'll stay a while longer."

I thanked Brenda and said my goodbye's to everyone and we left.

"Are you okay?" Monica asked as we raced across the bridge in the rain.

It was pouring down now, the wind whipping through our hair.

"I'm just tired, and have a lot on my mind after today."

"I'm sure Stewart doesn't know Avery's involved in money laundering."

"Even if he's not, he's giving him money for something, and it's not to board a dog."

"You need to tell Ben so he can sort it all out."

"I know."

Thunder cracked, and rain blew sideways, pelting us. "Hurry!" Monica shouted.

"Run ahead," I told her. My knee felt worlds better, but I was never a good runner. Running and breathing are two things I can't do at the same time, like walking and chewing gum.

A pickup pulled up beside us and stopped. "Get in," Quinn shouted from the window.

We climbed inside the warm, dry cab and closed out the wind and rain. "Perfect timing," Monica said.

"I saw you bolting down the boithrin and couldn't believe my eyes. What are you doing out in this? It's bucketing down."

"Coming back from a Halloween party," she said, grinning up at him.

He grinned back. "Looks as if you had a craic time of it."

"If that means it was fun, then yes," she said.

"Good." He leaned forward to see me around Monica. "You're quiet," he said. "Did you have fun as well?"

"I did. I'm tired, that's all. Thanks for asking."

Home was only the distance of a football field away, but it was nice not having to run in the rain. The lovebirds beside me snuggled together as I stared out into the dark night, feeling more alone than I had in a long time. I was losing Monica just as I got her back, Mom would be leaving again, and Ben and I . . . who knew what would happen with us.

All night I'd been surrounded by friends and family, but I was apart somehow. My mind hadn't been in the present, it had been busy worrying over Stewart and what to do about him. Maybe I should come right out and ask him what he was up to?

The pickup pulled in the driveway and lurched to a stop. "I think I'm going to go with Quinn," Monica said, but she didn't specify where or if she'd be home tonight. She was an adult, though, so I didn't question her.

"Have a good night," I said, slipping down from the cab and shutting the door.

I slogged across the driveway and down the sidewalk, past the beehive to the porch. Even the bees were tucked in tight together in their rain-proof box for the night.

I opened the door and was pummeled by twelve paws and three slobbery tongues giving doggy kisses. Immediately, my spirit lifted. "What would I do without you guys?" I got down on my knees and snuggled my face into Gus's fur, capturing a twin under each arm to hug.

"You've only been gone an hour," Mia said, standing at the end of the hall in the kitchen.

"We said it would be quick, and I didn't really feel like staying longer."

"Oh. Well, I called everybody who signed up for the pageant and told them about the parade. I didn't know where you wanted them to meet or what time, so I just told them to meet at the gristmill Sunday at noon."

"Mia, that's so kind of you. Thank you." I couldn't believe my ears. This girl had a huge heart when she wanted to. As soon as she grew out of her teen drama years, she would be a nice, thoughtful young woman.

She shrugged. "I was bored."

I watched her disappear back into the family room and couldn't help laughing silently to myself. What a kid.

· Eighteen ·

I woke up to Ben shaking me. "Cam, get up. The canal's flooding."

I bolted upright in bed. "No. It can't be. Not today."

"I'm sorry, but it is. It's headed this way."

I knew what that meant. Sand bags and lots of them. We had them stashed in the shed and the garage. "I'm getting up."

"Where's Monica? I knocked on her door, too."

"With Quinn."

"Oh. I see. It's serious with them then."

"Seems to be."

My clock read 4:38 in the morning. There was still a chance that the rain would stop and the flooding would go down in time for the festival. A slim chance, but a chance nonetheless.

Ben left me to get started outside. I staggered out of bed and stuck one foot and then the next into the jeans I wore to Brenda's party. After throwing on an old sweatshirt that hadn't been yarned with spaghetti and meatballs, I tugged on a pair of socks and stuck my feet into my rain boots.

Downstairs, Mia was shoving her arms into her raincoat. "I can't believe this is happening after I spent last night organizing a pet parade."

"Welcome to my world." I grabbed my own raincoat from the closet and pulled it on. "Let's go lug some sand around to the front of the house. They're heavy, so we'll work together."

"Too bad the dogs can't drag them."

"They'd have to be trained to do that, and they don't even sit on command."

"We really need to do something about them," she said, swinging the back door open to the lashing rain.

All five dogs were cowering in the corner beside the fridge, infringing on Isobel's private spot. She bared her teeth in annoyance. Even Spook was hiding out on top of my cupboards, peering down at the canine crew below.

"Bunch of wimps," I told them, stepping out into the storm and pulling the door closed.

The town was out in full force. Will, John, and Paul were securing the antiques that Will stored in his pole barn out back. "Good to see you two jailbirds!" I called over the rain, waving.

"Even in the rain it's a good day," John called back.

"In the canal town of Metamora, the community rallies together to overcome Mother Nature," Andy was saying while he filmed, standing in front of the garage.

"Already back at it, I see," I said, running up to give him a hug.

"This is award-winning material," he said. "The plight of man. Neighbors overcoming adversity."

"Well don't let me get in your way. We have sandbags to pile."

Mia and I each grabbed an end and hefted a bag off the ground a few inches. It was slow going, but we managed to get it to the end of the driveway. "Leave that there," Stewart said, jogging over. "Ben and I will stack them."

The canal had already risen over the banks and was halfway to the street. "I haven't listened to a weather report. Is it supposed to stop?"

"Not until tomorrow," he said, reaching up to squeeze my shoulder. "Sorry about Canal Days, Cam. I know how hard you worked on it."

"Yeah. Thanks." My heart was melting. All the time and effort my team and I put in was wasted. Gone in a flash flood.

Mia and I continued hauling sand bags to the end of the driveway for the next hour. Quinn pulled up with Monica in his pickup truck. "Judy woke us up to tell us about the flood," Monica shouted from the passenger side. Conan was cuddled against her side.

"I'm going to park on higher ground," Quinn said, "and come help."

Monica and Conan jumped out of the truck and ran around to the driveway while Quinn turned around and headed back up the street to find a safe place to park.

"Looks like you've made a new friend," I said, patting Conan's head.

"He's the best dog. Smarter than a lot of people," she said, chuckling.

"Maybe that'll rub off on the others."

We looked at each other, shared a doubtful look with Mia, and all three of us laughed. My dogs were hopeless.

A second automobile pulled up in front of the house, this time a car. A car with Nick Valentine inside. "Don't get mad," he said, darting out from the driver's side. "I'm not here to see Mia. I need to see Officer Hayman. I need help." He looked over his shoulder. "Avery Bantum is trying to kill me."

∞

"What do you mean Avery Bantum is trying to kill you?" I'd made Nick come inside, sat him down at the kitchen table, and gotten him a cup of strong coffee.

"We've been trying to find out what he had to do with Butch Landow's death," Mia said to me.

I spun to her. "What?! What do you mean *we?*"

"Well, you and your Action Agency never include me in anything, so when I ran into Nick and we started talking and he told me his boss was into some dirty business, I figured I'd find out what and make you and Dad proud of me."

My stomach sank. "Mia, we're always proud of you. You don't have to solve a murder to make us proud. You put yourself in serious danger."

Nick drummed his fingers on the table. "Avery found out I was snooping around at work. I told him I don't know anything, but he pulled a gun on me and said I know too much. I ran. He fired shots but missed me."

"Good gravy. How do we get you out of this mess?"

"Shouldn't we get Dad?" Mia asked.

"Of course we should. Just not right this second." I needed to find out how Stewart figured in to this, but not with Mia sitting here. "Do you know what Avery is up to?" I asked Nick instead.

"Not the exact details, but he's been getting a lot of money from people and not from keeping their dogs at the kennel. There's never one dog in there."

"What do you do there then?"

"Mostly he has me watching the security cameras and letting him know if anyone shows up."

"He's shady," Mia said.

"So this is what you two have been up to?" I asked.

"I told you it wasn't what you thought," Mia said. "I was trying to help and you grounded me from the pageant."

"You were sneaking around doing something dangerous. I don't feel bad about grounding you." I turned back to Nick. "Do you know what Track Times is?"

He shook his head. "I've been trying to find out. I know it has something to do with all the cash."

I took a deep breath, resigning myself to what I had to do next—get Ben and Stewart inside and lay everything out on the table. "I'm going to get your dad," I told Mia. "You and Nick stay here."

"Are you going to tell him I was involved?" she asked, pleading.

"Mia, I just don't know if I can keep it from him."

She closed her eyes and let out a huff.

"We'll see," I said. "Let's get Nick out of trouble and then we'll worry about you."

∞

Back outside, Monica and Quinn had joined Ben and Stewart stacking sand bags. Will, John, and Paul were now doing the same next door. Conan dragged a bag down the driveway toward the street. There was nothing that dog couldn't do. All of them were soaked to the bone, and a low, lumpy wall was going up slowly, but surely. A wall that Mike stood on top of, quacking like a drill sergeant.

"Ben!" I shouted. "Ben! I need to talk to you! It's urgent!"

"If it's about Elaina, we're headed her way next," he called back.

"Elaina? What's wrong with Elaina?"

"She's having some crisis or another."

"I'll head over there now!" It terrified me to think of our own Grandma Diggity in trouble.

The streets were flooding, so I couldn't take Monica's car. I high-tailed it as fast as my legs would carry me to the bridge. The water was rushing underneath so close to the boards of the bridge, I was afraid it might wash away. With no time to let fear derail me, I kept on going and ran down the ally past Read and ReRead to the next road, where Elaina's house sat on the corner.

Sue and Elaina sat on the screened in porch. Sue was trying to calm her grandma. "It's okay, we'll find him."

"Find who?" I asked, rushing inside. "Ben said there was something going on."

"Good Luck Chuck!" Elaina howled, crying and balling her shirt in her fists. "He's stuck in the barn. We have to get to him before it floods!"

"Who's Good Luck Chuck?" I asked.

Sue shook her head, clearly as confused as I was.

"Elaina," I said, taking her hand and easing her balled up shirt out of her fist. "Tell me who Good Luck Chuck is. Where does he live?"

"In the barn! In the barn!"

"Okay, is he a horse?"

"No! He's Good Luck Chuck!"

"We're getting nowhere fast," Sue said. "Grandma, is Chuck a person or an animal?"

"Why would he be a person? How could a person run that fast?"

An animal that ran fast. "Not a horse?"

"Good Luck Chuck isn't a horse!" Elaina shouted. "Butch sold all his horses!"

"Butch? Butch Landow? Good Luck Chuck was his? And he's in his barn?"

"He's stuck in the barn! I can't get him!"

"Good gravy, come on, Sue! We have a ... a *something* to save."

"Don't worry, Grandma, Cam and I will get Chuck out of the barn. You stay here. We'll be right back, okay?"

"Poor Chuck," Elaina whimpered.

Sue pulled her phone out. "I'm texting Steph to come stay with her and make sure she doesn't wander out in the storm."

We hurried out the door of Elaina's porch and jogged down the road that ran behind Dog Diggity. The electric fence may or may not have been turned off. I never did get the answer I'd been searching for, but either way, the two of us had to get past it onto Landow farm land.

"Let me," I said, stopping her from reaching out and touching the wire. "If I die, don't let my mother bury me in pink."

"I promise," she said.

I squinted my eyes and quickly jabbed my forefinger against the wire.

Nothing.

"Oh, thank the lord." I pressed my hand to my battering heart.

"Let's go through," Sue said, holding the top wire up and stepping over the bottom one. "Careful, these are barbed."

I knew me, and I knew my luck, so I wasn't at all surprised when my hair snagged on the upper wire, and the rubber sole of my rain boot got impaled on the bottom.

"We have to get moving," Sue said, already jogging away from the fence.

I did what any good town employee would do in an emergency, and bucked up, jerking my head through and losing a boot. I kicked off the other boot and ran, rubbing my head where I'd sacrificed quite a few strands of hair. It hurt like Hades's fire.

"Do you know this farm?" I yelled to Sue.

"No, do you?"

"No. How do we find the barn?"

"Should be close to the house."

185

It made sense, but I didn't remember seeing it in Andy's video.

I followed her down a hill that curved to the right and around a patch of trees. The ground was worn into a path, and I kept slipping in mud. My socks dragged six inches off of each of my feet, throwing up wet splotches of mud into my face as I ran. I could barely see for the rain in my eyes. So help me, if I got to this barn and nobody was inside in need of saving, Grandma Diggity was toast.

Despite the adrenaline rush pumping through me, I was panting and light headed. I wasn't used to running like this. I never wanted to be used to it, either. Why run when you can walk? That was my motto. And even though the rain had finally broken through the clouds, my knee wasn't back to one hundred percent.

I had to stop before I busted a lung. "Sue!" I yelled between gasps of air. I bent over and braced my hands on my knees. "I've gotta...slow... down."

She jogged back to me. "Want me to go on ahead?"

I nodded, holding up a finger. "Just need one minute to catch my breath. I'll catch up."

Sue dashed off again and disappeared around a bend up ahead between the trees. Glancing down I realized I was standing in a puddle that covered my left foot completely. Giving up on the socks, I peeled them off and tossed them aside. Mud squished between my toes—and probably worms, but I didn't let my thoughts linger on that. I had to get moving again.

I started out walking, picking up the pace as I went, ramping up slowly, only as much as my lung capacity would allow. I didn't want to end up gasping again. Maybe I had exercise-induced asthma?

Who was I kidding? I didn't normally exercise enough to induce a sweat, let alone asthma.

Good gravy, I was out of shape.

Where was this barn?

A low whine sounded from behind me in the distance, but it was getting closer. An engine. Who in the world would be out in this storm driving around the back pasture of Landow Farm?

Nothing good could come of this.

I hustled in between two holly bushes and waited to see who would pass by. A four-wheeler came into view with a man riding it. He slowed as he reached the puddle I'd stopped and rested in.

My socks! He saw them! The man on a four-wheeler got off and approached one of my discarded socks. I couldn't tell who he was because of his helmet, but he was average-sized, if not a bit on the tall side. I didn't recognize him from his build or his clothes: jeans and a black nylon jacket.

But when he reached down and snatched up one of my socks, I saw the gold pinkie ring flashing on his finger.

Arnie Rutherford!

· Nineteen ·

$\mathcal{I}$'d been on the right track all along! I knew he was a shady character. There was his past, of course, when he'd been busted for overpricing his home sales and pocketing the difference, but that wasn't the only reason I was leery of him. He'd warned me away from asking questions and trying to dig up information about Butch Landow's death. That spurred instant suspicion. Now here he was.

But what was I supposed to do about him? Stay hidden in the bushes? He knew I—or someone—was close. He was holding my sock for Pete's sake.

Quack! I jumped about a foot in the air. Metamora Mike stood behind me, eyeing me with his beady little black eyes. *Quack!*

"Go away!" I whispered, rather loudly, but hoping the hum of the idling four-wheeler would keep Arnie from hearing me. "I don't have any treats!" I waved my arms at him, trying to shoo him away.

"Mrs. Hayman," Arnie said, "is that you?"

I turned back around, cursing that darn duck under my breath. And I waved.

Really, at that point, what else could I do?

"Hello, Mr. Rutherford. What brings you out in this weather?"

As if on queue, thunder rumbled overhead.

"I was going to ask you the same. Do you need a ride somewhere?"

Both of us avoided the real question: *What are* you *doing* here?

Knowing it was foolish, I did what any irrational freshman college girl in Daytona on Spring Break would do—certainly not what a level-headed, forty-year-old woman would—and said, "I would like a ride if you're offering."

Ben flashed before my eyes, scowling and asking me if I had a death wish.

I shoved him aside. *The man was afraid of the dark basement for cripes' sake,* I thought, trying to justify getting on a four-wheeler with a potential—okay, a probable—killer.

Quickly, I gave myself reasons I was accepting his offer. 1) He'd never threatened me in any way, and B) I was wet and cold and tired and my lungs hurt. Thirdly, if I was ever going to get to the bottom of who killed Butch, I had to follow this lead, wherever it may ... well, lead.

Like a gentleman, Arnie handed me his helmet to use. I tugged it onto my head and sat astride the four-wheeler behind him. "Hang on," he said. "I'll go slow, but the seat's slippery."

It was a bit awkward hanging on to a man I barely knew, but when the wheels dug in and the mud started flying, I got over it fast. We rounded the bend where Sue had run ahead. As soon as we caught up to her and I wasn't alone with Arnie, I'd feel a million times better about this situation. But before too long, a major problem arose.

A fork in the path.

Arnie went left. I had no idea which direction Sue had gone. The odds were good—50/50 to be exact—that I wouldn't be catching up with her at all.

Good gravy, why did I let that freshman spring break girl inside my head talk me into this? This had to be Mia's influence in my life. I was channeling a teenager's ability to reason.

Lightning struck too close for comfort, sending up sparks from a stand of trees about thirty yards away.

Canal Days and Elaina's polka dots hadn't killed me, but Arnie or Mother Nature might.

The path curved to the left and opened up into a wide stretch of field. Straight ahead sat a red barn. Sue was nowhere in sight.

Arnie sped around the barn to the front, where a pair of doors stood open. I could barely make out another person moving around inside. Someone tall. A man.

The four-wheeler stopped and so did my heart. The man inside was Avery Bantum. Something inside me was telling me to run and run fast. Maybe it was that freshman college girl who got me into this, shouting, *Get out of here, Cameron!* These two men together were double the trouble.

Arnie stood and swung his leg over the seat, getting off the four-wheeler. Instinct took over, and even though I'd never driven one before, I slid forward, turned the key, and twisted the hand throttle.

The knobby tires jumped off the ground and the thing leapt forward like a wild cat. I barely hung on. Behind me, Arnie was yelling for me to stop.

The wind raced by and rain lashed my face. I couldn't see very far ahead and my eyes were blinking like a turn signal on the fritz. I hit a divot in the ground and the ATV lurched to the left, sending half of me off of the seat. I struggled to right myself and kept going. How could anybody think this was fun?

The open field narrowed and trees encroached from the right. I followed narrowing land, not slowing a bit to let them catch up.

Avery had gotten himself to that barn somehow, and for all I knew, they were on my tail on another ATV or riding a tractor or in a truck.

Keeping the throttle twisted, I soldiered on, wondering where I'd end up. Where was Butch's house on this property? Where was Sue?

Without warning, the ground dropped out from under me and I was flying through the air. Good gravy! I'd been at the top of a hill and hadn't known it until I shot off of it at top speed. How was I going to land this thing without breaking my neck?

Every muscle in my body constricted, hanging on for dear life. I was dropping down fast, the ground rising to crush me. I let out a whimper of fear, the best I could do while holding my breath, and closed my eyes. I made several quick promises—if I made it through this I'd never eat another cookie, I'd never get frustrated with Mia, I'd never ... Oh who was I kidding? I couldn't keep those promises.

I landed with a teeth-rattling thud. The lumpy tires bounced a few times, jolting me off the seat. My hand still gripped the accelerator, holding on for all I was worth and thus sending me speeding downhill. My brain couldn't catch up with my body to tell it what to do, like *slow down!*

At the bottom of the hill, there was a fenced area with rickety wooden stands, like bleachers. Inside was an oval track. For all the world it looked like a peewee football field. Why would Butch have a peewee football field on his farm?

I got closer and finally pried my fingers from the throttle, eventually coming to a stop. I'd never been so eager to get off of something in my life, not even the time I let Monica talk me into riding the biggest roller coaster at Cedar Point. Although, that was a close second.

I walked up to the fence surrounding the track. It was flooded and muddy. Another low fence ran along the inside of the track. At the far end before the turn sat a low row of gates, like those I saw at the horse racing track, but these were smaller, closer to the ground. A horse would never fit behind or between them.

What on earth was going on here? Miniature pony racing? Did people race Shetlands? Did Butch own one? He might not have bet on horses, but he had his own track right on his farm.

A track… Track Times! It wasn't the name of a newspaper or magazine, like *The New York Times*. Why didn't it come to me before? Track Times had something to do with racing, and Butch was in debt to them so much he willed them his farm. Or did he? Certainly he wouldn't have known he was going to be murdered. If he'd changed his will to give his land to Track Times upon his death and then committed suicide, freeing him of his debt… and his life… well, it would be drastic, but it made more sense.

Unless Track Times, which Avery Bantum made large bank deposits to, was *owned* by Avery, and the will was a fake. Arnie Rutherford knew his way around fake contracts and documents; he'd been arrested for fraud in the past. Did they set this all up? Did they kill Butch?

One thing was certain, I had to get out of here fast.

I hopped back on the four-wheeler and turned the key.

Nothing happened.

Good gravy, what if I had to prime the engine or do who knew what to get it started? I was terrible with this kind of thing. It was a good day when I could get the lawn mower going, which was why Andy had been such a blessing.

I twisted the throttle a few times, then turned the key. Not a sound, nothing but a faint smell of gasoline. Had I flooded the engine? Did I break the whole thing taking that hill like Evel Knievel?

With no other choice, I got off and started running. There was no way I'd make it back up that hill, and no way I'd go back toward the barn, so I rounded the track and took my chances with what was on the other side.

The water ran off of the track in the same direction I was jogging, so I figured it must be all downhill from here. Figuratively and literally.

A path ran through a thin outcrop of trees. It was rocky and rutted. The slippery mud made it even more hazardous, not to mention I was hoofing it in bare feet. There was no running or jogging, or even walking fast. I picked my way over exposed tree roots and rivulets of running rain water. In the distance down below, I could just make out the roofline of a house through the treetops.

The rain was slowing, and the sky was growing lighter. A bird chirruped overhead. Then I caught another sound. The whine of a small but powerful engine. The four-wheeler!

I tried to hurry, but the rocks were sharp and my feet were sinking in the mud. Whoever was behind me was gaining. The engine grew louder and louder with every passing second. I had to get off the path and hide.

"Look at you."

I startled at Arnie's voice. He stood at the bottom of the pitted trail. It must be Avery coming up behind me.

"Mud up to your neck," he said. "No shoes, and you didn't have the good sense to take that helmet off your head. What a sight you are."

I reached up and patted the sides of the helmet. I hadn't even realized I'd still been wearing it. Not that I would've wasted the few seconds it took to take it off. But as he neared, I thought maybe it was a good thing I still had it on.

I kept quiet and waited for him to get closer.

"What made you run, Mrs. Hayman? I thought we were friends. I did give you that warning about digging up information on this place, after all." He laughed. It was deep and threatening, like some evil villain from a cartoon. "You need to learn to keep your nose out of things that aren't your business," he continued, taking one more step closer, as close as I needed him to be.

I whipped the helmet off my head and swung it with all my might, striking him in the side of his face. He wobbled, and I took off down the path. He had to have driven *something* to Butch's house to get in front of me so quickly on my way from the barn. I was hoping it was a vehicle this time and not another ATV.

But Avery was still fast approaching. I heard the whine of the engine slow and dared a peek back over my shoulder. He was astride the four-wheeler I'd been unable to get restarted at the track, stopped next to Arnie. Arnie hopped on the back and they took off after me again.

I darted into the trees, racing over rocks and stones and sticks and tree roots. Sharp pains shot through the bottoms of my feet, but I didn't have time to worry about it. If I could still run, I was going to run, no matter the shape of the soles of my feet.

My only hope was that the trees would be close enough together to stop them from getting me. So far, they'd had to take a different route through the trees, but they still had sight of me. It was enough to keep distance between us.

I descended the hill, planning my next move. I didn't have the stamina to keep running much longer. My only hope was getting inside the house and calling for help. But what if it was locked? What if there was no phone.

Good gravy, what a time to leave home without my handbag with my cell phone tucked all snug inside one of its many voluminous pockets.

There was nothing I could do but take a chance and head for the house.

I broke left and darted through a briar patch I hadn't seen. There was no stopping, and I had a good feeling I was bleeding. If Avery and Arnie caught me, they'd harm me a lot more than those briars.

I broke right and bobbed and weaved through a few low branches with the footwork of a professional boxer. Float like a butterfly, sting like a bee.

A few yards ahead there was a path between the trees that led straight down to the house. I took a deep breath and sprinted downhill, gathering speed like a snowball in an avalanche.

My top half started to go faster than my feet. Gravity was a jokester, apparently. I took longer strides, but my legs just wouldn't go any faster. Losing balance, I wheeled my arms backwards, hoping to stop myself with wind resistance, I guess.

Who was I kidding? It was just instinct. I couldn't think of anything at that moment other than, *Good gravy, I'm going tail over teakettle!*

Which was exactly what happened.

The ground came up and I went down, tumbling and somersaulting to the bitter bottom of the hill. I should've left my helmet on, because the last roll was a doozy. I whacked the back of my head on a large rock hard enough to bring tears to my eyes.

I lay there for a second or two, until I could see straight again. Then I slowly stood, staggering with dizziness. On my left, Arnie and Avery were hurtling through the trees. On my right, flashing red and blue lights speeding up Butch's driveway.

It was Metamora One.

Ben.

The world spun. The earth tilted, and I went down, falling into blackness.

· Twenty ·

$\mathcal{I}$ don't know how long I was out, but when I opened my eyes, Roy was staring down at me and Brutus licked my face. "Ya went down like a sack of potatoes, Cameron Cripps-Hayman."

"Thanks, Roy." I lifted my head to get up, but there were hands on my shoulders holding me down.

"Stay still now," Johnna said, kneeling behind me. "I've never seen a goose egg that big before."

"That's one nasty bump you got there," Roy agreed.

"Where's Ben?" I asked. "What are you two doing here?"

"Ben's reading Arnie Rutherford and Avery Bantum their rights," Nick said.

I turned my head to find him standing a few feet away beside Mia, who was white as a sheet with her eyes locked on me. "Mia," I said, "are you okay?"

"I thought you were dead," she whispered. "When we got here. I thought—"

"Shh," Nick whispered, "she's not. She's fine."

I saw the look of compassion he gave her, and knew she was right. Nick wasn't a bad guy despite outward appearances and the assault charge he'd landed himself in the past for fighting.

"Ben figured there was trouble," Roy said. "Nick told him what he knew, and Johnna and I had been checking on Elaina when Sue came running in like her pants were on fire. Once we told Ben, he told us all to get in his truck and here we are."

"There's a dog track," I said, delicately prodding my head to feel the giant lump. "Over that hill. Track Times must be owned by Avery and Arnie. That's who Butch owed. That's who got his house when he died."

"Dollars to donuts they killed him," Johnna said.

"With Arnie's past, he'd know how to forge Butch's will, too," I said.

She squeezed my shoulders as she thought about it. "I told ya he was guilty as sin."

"Okay, okay. Let go." I reached up and pried her fingers loose but stayed on the soggy ground. At least the rain had stopped.

A medic from Brookville came over with a bag of equipment to check me over, shooing Brutus, Johnna, and Roy out of the way. She took my vitals and pronounced that I had a concussion and several lacerations on my feet and legs. But other than the scrapes, bumps, and bruises, I was fine.

She helped me sit up just in time to see Sheriff Reins arrive in the big white cruiser that always reminded me of a whale. He and Ben spoke, and then Arnie and Avery were put in the back of Reins's car.

My whole body ached and I was exhausted, but I had to get up. The grass was spongey with water and I'd been lying in it for I didn't know how long. The medic helped me stand, and I let her know I was fine.

"Mia," I said and motioned for her to come to me.

She walked over, hesitant, like my shakiness was an indication of my imminent demise. "I'm fine," I told her, pulling her in for a hug. "I just need to take it easy for a day or two and I'll be back to normal."

She hugged me tight and nodded against my shoulder but didn't say anything. This had really freaked her out.

"Cam!" Monica shouted.

I turned to find her running across Butch's backyard toward me. Quinn, with Conan at his side, and Mom, Sue, and Elaina trailed behind her. She reached Mia and me and threw her arms around us both. "I was so worried!"

"You know," Roy said, sauntering up to us, "we never had this trouble until you came to town, missy."

Monica shot him an indignant look. "Don't you have a barstool to be on?"

He pointed to his eyes and then to Monica, letting her know he was watching her.

Sue came up and shook her head. "I'm so sorry I couldn't find you. I figured I better go back and find help."

"I'm glad you did, or we would both be in a world of hurt right now," I told her. "Ben got here just in time."

Elaina was regaling Quinn with pleas. "What kind of dog lover are you? Good Luck Chuck needs saved!"

"Chuck's a dog!" I said. "Of course! Dog racing!"

"He's in the barn!" Elaina yelled.

"You wouldn't happen to have seen the barn?" Sue asked. "This is all I've heard since this morning from her."

I pointed up the hill. "At the top of this incline there's a dog track with another hill on the other side of it. At the top of that there's a barn."

"Or we could just drive around to the farm workers' entrance," Roy said, raising his brow and looking smug.

"Let's do that," I said, wincing as I took a step forward.

"You should stay here," Monica said, putting an arm around me.

"Not a chance. I came this far, I'm seeing this through."

I hobbled to the driveway with the help of my friends and family. Ben rushed to my side. "What are you doing? You need to be resting. I'll take you home."

"I'm fine. There's a dog in the barn. We're going to rescue him."

"You're not thinking of bringing another dog into the house, are you?" Panic flitted across his face, and I couldn't help but chuckle.

"We'll see. One of us will have to take him."

"Reins is taking Avery and Arnie to the station. I'll go with you."

Our ever growing crew grew larger as two more cars pulled into the driveway. Logan and Anna in one, and Carl Finch in another.

"We heard something was going on," Anna said, tugging Logan along by the hand. This kind of situation gave him hives. He's the agency's research guy, staying nice and safe behind his computer monitor.

Roy filled them in while Carl sidled up to Mom, giving her a kiss on the cheek.

I glanced around me. My mom and sister fit right in with my friends and Action Agency members, which, with Nick here, was like having the old band back together. They'd rushed to my rescue, propped me up when I couldn't stand on my own, and now they were dashing off to save another. Looking back, my life before moving here four years ago was empty. Sure, I had co-workers and a few friends I went to dinner with every now and then, but nothing like this. Metamora and the people who lived here had more heart and soul than anywhere I could ever imagine. And they'd taken me in as one of their own.

We piled into the cars, Ben helping me up into the passenger's seat of Metamora One with Brutus in the center between us, tongue lolling and a doggie smile stretching his lips. Roy and Johnna rode with Sue and Elaina, and Mia and Nick rode with Monica, Conan, and Quinn.

All the cars pulled out, Sue in the lead with Roy giving directions, I assumed. Metamora One brought up the end of our parade down the driveway and around the corner to the farm entrance.

A bumpy lane led back to the side of the barn I hadn't ventured upon during my ATV exploits. We all piled out and rounded the barn to the front where the doors still stood open.

"Chuck!" Elaina called. "Chuck, where are you?"

A scuffing sound came from a horse stall in the back corner of the barn. Elaina rushed toward it with Sue right behind her. They flung the door open and there he was, Good Luck Chuck. The white dog with reddish-tan splotches on his sides and haunches looked up at us. A muzzle was fastened around his head and his ears sat flat.

Elaina reached for the buckle to unfasten the muzzle.

"Wait," Quinn said. "Let me. We don't know his temperament."

Everyone stepped back to let Quinn pass into the stall. He shut the door and patted the dog on the back. Chuck shivered and quaked, retreating backward.

"It's okay," Quinn told him, calmly, kneeling down. "There's a good lad. What did those chancers do to ya?"

He slowly reached over and unbuckled the muzzle, pulling it off gently. The dog skittered away from him, cowering in the corner.

"What's wrong with him?" Johnna asked, peering over the top of the stall.

"He's afraid," Monica said. "I wonder how long he's been in here."

"Doesn't look ill treated," Roy said. "Looks fed. No fleas."

"Probably just not socialized," I said. "He doesn't look like he's used to people."

Johnna opened the door and waltzed inside the stall.

"Careful," Quinn warned.

"He's not gonna hurt me. Come here, love," she said, pulling a few feet of highlighter-yellow knitted yarn from her tote bag. "Johnna has something to keep you warm." She went right up to him and wrapped her half-kitted project around his middle. "There you go." She patted his head, and he licked her hand. "You come on home with me. Johnna will make sure you're taken care of."

Beside me, Ben sighed in relief. I had to agree with him, my house was at max canine capacity.

Conan nudged the swinging stall door open with his nose and eased inside. He padded over to Chuck's side and sat, like an assigned protector. Brutus followed, mocking Conan's actions and sitting on Chuck's other side.

Quinn laughed. "The Three Stooges."

We all had a good chuckle watching them, big burly Brutus; tall, sleek, and intelligent Conan; and their new friend, Chuck, who all of us would get to know soon.

"Mom," Sue said, "how did you know Chuck was in here?"

"He's a sure bet," Elaina said. "Good Luck Chuck to win!"

"You knew Butch had dog races here?"

"Who didn't?" the old woman asked.

It stood to reason that when you've lived in a town for nine decades you'd probably know everything that went on. I'd have to keep that in mind next time I was digging up information.

Johnna tied a string of bubblegum pink yarn around Chuck's neck like a leash. "Let's go home, sweet boy. You need a bath and some nice warm chicken soup."

"Can dogs eat chicken soup?" I whispered to Monica.

"As long as there are no onions or garlic in it. I'll make sure she knows what to avoid."

"Guess you have another treat tester."

"You and our friends need to stop rescuing dogs! At this rate, every dog in town will be a tester and I won't have anyone left to sell them to."

"I doubt we'll end up with *every* dog in town."

Monica smiled, shaking her head. "I'll remind you that you said that."

Johnna led the still-quaking Chuck out of the stall. We all gave him a wide berth. He kept his head down and ears back, but didn't try to run away or snap at us.

"I've got an extra lead in my truck," Quinn offered.

"We prefer the softness of cashmere yarn," Johnna said, striding with her new companion to the barn doors. "Who's taking us home?"

I held back a chuckle. In true Johnna kleptomaniac fashion, she'd strolled in and claimed the dog as her own. It was another match made in Metamora, like Monica and Quinn, and Mom and Carl. Only time would tell if those matches were made in heaven.

∞

After Ben drove us home, I took a bath and Mia helped me get comfortable on the couch, bringing me warm tea and magazines. Ben had to go down to the station to follow up on Arnie and Avery's arrest and file paperwork, so Mom and Monica hovered.

"We can't let her fall asleep," Mom insisted. "Let's watch a movie or something."

"That's a myth," Mia said, showing Mom a webpage on her cell phone. "She can sleep as long as she can hold a conversation, and TV is actually bad for her."

Mom harumphed. "I'll make her a sandwich. She can still eat, can't she?"

"Yes, but nothing spicy. She might get nauseous."

Mia, my little caretaker. I took her hand. "Thank you for taking care of me."

Monica whisked into the family room with a blanket and my bed pillow. "Lift your head," she said, tucking the pillow behind me. "I'm sleeping in your room tonight to keep an eye on you."

"I'm fine. Really."

Liam hopped up and snuggled in between my ankles. Fiddle and Faddle had parked it in front of the fireplace, clueless to the world, and Gus paced around the coffee table, sensing something was wrong but not knowing what. Isobel ignored all of us, of course, and snoozed in her spot beside the refrigerator.

"I need my planner and my cell phone, Mon," I said.

"For what?"

"I need to call Soapy and figure out what to do about Canal Days. We need to get word out." The streets were still under a few inches of standing water when we drove home from Landow Farm. The sandbags were keeping the canal from encroaching on our side of the street, though, and so far my front yard was soaked from the rain but not suffering a flood.

"You'll do no such thing," Mom called from the kitchen. "Soapy can take care of it."

"I'll call him and tell him what happened," Mia offered. "If he needs help, I'll get with the Action Agency and we'll take care of it."

"Are you sure? I feel terrible leaving it up to you and everyone else."

"Have you seen your head?" she asked. "You look like one of those gray aliens on that show Dad likes to watch. You're in no shape to do anything but lay here."

I frowned, and Gus sneaked up and gave my face a lick. He looked me over and whined. "You think I look like an alien, too, huh?" I asked him.

He licked me again.

Mia went off to call Soapy. Mom brought me a peanut butter and jelly sandwich, and Monica sat in the rocking chair, looking melancholy. "What's wrong?" I asked her, between bites of my sticky sandwich.

She gazed out the window as she answered. "Did you see how good Quinn was with Chuck today?"

"Yeah, he's great with dogs."

"He's great with everything. It's not fair."

"You're great at things, too, you know."

"No, I don't mean—it's not fair that he has to leave!"

"Oh, I see what you mean. No, it's not fair, Mon."

"I'm not so young anymore. I don't have forever to get married if I want to have a baby. And the guy I'm crazy about lives in Ireland. Why did this have to happen?"

"Would you rather it didn't? Would you rather have never met him?"

She shook her head. "No. I just wish … I don't know. I wish we could be together somehow."

"I know." I didn't know what else to say. There was nothing I could offer that would make the situation any less heartbreaking. When Quinn left Metamora, Monica's heart would go with him. It would take her a long, long time to get over him, if she ever did.

"He asked me if I'd ever move to Ireland," she said, knocking me for a loop.

"What? You can't! I mean, you wouldn't, would you?"

"I don't know, Cam. I don't want to. The thought of moving to a country I've never even visited is terrifying. It wouldn't be right away. We only just met after all. It's hard to imagine going that far. But it's hard to imagine losing him, too."

I took a sip of tea, washing down the peanut butter. "Try not to think about it. Enjoy your time with him, and it'll work itself out."

"How?"

"Somehow. Things always work out somehow."

The front door squeaked open and I heard Ben's work boots treading down the hall. He came around the corner into the kitchen and saw me sitting on the family room couch. "Why aren't you in bed sleeping?"

"I'm perfectly fine here, and I just ate a sandwich."

"You need to rest."

"What does it look like I'm doing? A three-legged relay race?"

He sat on the edge of the couch looking down at me. "No matter how many times I ask you to stay out of police business, you're not going to, are you?"

"Not when I'm the one who finds them and my friends or my family are suspects."

"Okay, then I'm going to revise my plea. Can you please stop finding dead bodies?"

"I'll do my best. Promise."

He bent down and kissed my forehead. "Arnie sang like a canary in the interrogation room."

"He did? What did he say?"

"Well, once we promised to be lenient when considering his past arrest, he told us he was in serious debt to Avery, and Avery told him if he forged a will they'd call it even."

"Butch's will. I knew it!"

"Yes, but then Avery blackmailed Arnie. If Arnie didn't help get John and Paul, who conveniently wanted to buy Butch's farm, convicted of the murder, Avery would turn Arnie in for forging the will."

"So Arnie got in over his head."

"Way over his head."

"It's a slippery slope from fraud to murder, I guess."

Ben rubbed his cheek thoughtfully. "I don't think he knew Avery's plan to murder Butch, but that's for a judge and jury to decide."

"I'm just glad it's solved, and Andy, John, and Paul have their names cleared."

I snuggled down into my pillow, my stomach full, blanket warm, and feeling like I could barely keep my eyes open.

"I have one more question for you, and then I'll let you sleep," Ben said.

"Hmm?"

"Why were you barefoot?"

With my eyes closed, I smiled. "Long story."

"It always is with you," he said, chuckling.

· Twenty-One ·

A week had passed and the canal had receded back below its banks. The sky was bright and the air crisp, perfect fall weather. Vendors lined the streets on both sides of the canal; the Canal Days festivities were in full swing.

Dog Diggity was celebrating its grand opening after Andy had the week to finish the last projects he'd been working on. Old Dan pitched in as well.

The exterior got a fresh coat of white paint, and Monica hung a baby blue awning with orange polka dots across the front. The sign was in a curlicue font with a paw print dotting the *i*. Overall, the effect was adorable.

Stewart approached the Action Agency table that stood in front of Dog Diggity. "Here to buy some honey?" I asked, holding up a jar of the golden goodness.

"Absolutely." He handed me a five-dollar bill. "And I was wondering"—he glanced around and leaned in closer—"did you happen to find any betting books at Butch's farm?"

"Books with records of who bet and how much?" I asked, guessing he was nervous about finding his name written down on such a list. "No. But I didn't search around. I'm not sure what Ben and Reins might find."

He looked over my head and nodded distractedly. "Alright. Thanks for the honey."

"Stewart? I wouldn't worry about something you can't control. Nothing might ever be found."

He twisted his lips, considering, and nodded again before walking away from the table.

"Irene will have his hide if she finds out," Johnna said, knitting a scarf for Chuck, who lay curled in a ball at her feet, his belly stuffed with Monica's dog treats.

"Well, I'm not going to tell her."

Behind us, Dog Diggity was packed. A crowd of people milled around inside with treat bags in their hands. I hoped Monica sold out and we were up until midnight baking more treats for tomorrow.

In the past week, I'd gotten enough sleep and forced rest to last me a long while. The giant bump on my head had gone down to just a small lump that wasn't visible under my hair, and I felt fine. Better than fine, really.

Since we'd missed our movie date last week, Ben came over and read to me from *Sunset At Dawn*, the book that Cass raved about that the zombie movie we'd walked out of was based on. While it wasn't as great as Cass made it seem, it was a million times better than the sensationalized movie. The best part was Ben reading to me. He'd never done that before. It wasn't even something I'd ever imagine him doing. Whatever was going on between us, it was good. It was bringing us closer.

"You go on and walk around a bit," Johnna said, wrapping her needles and setting aside the yarn ball. "Chuck and I can hold down the fort."

I didn't doubt that they could, I only doubted her ability to keep her sticky fingers out of the till. "Maybe I'll do that. Roy should be back soon."

He'd gone to find a caramel apple. At least that's what he said. I had my suspicions that he'd escaped to the Cornerstone bar.

I strolled down the road, stopping at the Soapy Savant to get a cup of spiced cider from their cauldron. "I can smell that at my house," I told Theresa. "I wish it smelled that good every day."

"I have candles with a similar scent," she said.

"Think it'll cover eau de dog?"

"Couldn't hurt. I've got some over on the table." She gestured to where Soapy was manning their table of items for sale.

"I'll check it out," I said. I walked over, warming my hands on my paper cider cup. "Hey, Soapy."

"Cam! Feeling better?"

"One hundred percent." I picked up a candle and sniffed. Apple pie scent. My mouth watered.

"Turned out to be the perfect weather, didn't it?"

"Much better than last weekend, and the crowd is still pretty big."

"We've had a ton of customers come through. I think a lot of our neighbors are going to have a profitable weekend."

"Monica's been busy from the minute she opened her door. Honey sales are pretty good, too. I hope we get enough for new desks."

"About that. I have some bad news."

I picked up a cinnamon candle and sniffed. "I'm sorry, I'm closed for bad news today."

"The church was flooded really badly, Cam. I'm not sure when or even if you and your crew can get back down there and work."

I blinked. "Where will we go?"

"I'm working on it. Don't worry. We'll think of something."

It was bad news, but not terrible. Wherever we found to put down stakes couldn't be any worse than a moldy old church basement. "I'm sure it'll be fine," I said, giving him a confident smile. Soapy was good to us. He'd find somewhere for us to work.

I bought the cinnamon and apple pie candles and went on my way. A little farther down, Logan was perched on the ledge inside a dunk tank. I couldn't believe my eyes. "Logan, what are you doing in there?" I called to him.

"Fundraiser for the Number Ninjas," he shouted.

I figured that was his math club. I gave three dollars to the lady running the tank—one of the ninja's mom's, I imagined—and she gave me three softballs. "Okay, here goes nothing!"

"Don't you dare!" Logan yelled.

I threw and the ball went high.

A few people stopped to watch.

I wound up and threw the next one underhand. It missed by an inch to the outside of the target. "One more!" I called to Logan.

"Miss it!" he yelled back.

"You got this," a tall, gangly kid said. Another ninja?

I pulled my arm back, pointed at the target with my free hand and whipped the ball straight ahead. It hit the metal target with an echoing *thunk!* The platform fell out from under Logan and he splashed down in the tank of steamy warm water.

The crowd that had gathered cheered. Anna rushed up to me, laughing. We high-fived, and she took pictures with her phone. Logan didn't find it as amusing, but he took it with good nature. Since I'd sunk him, I got a Number Ninjas button. I thanked the mom in charge and tossed it in my bag with my candles.

I set off for my next stop at Sue's Soda Pop Shop. I told myself I would behave and not indulge in too many sweets, but her fudge was not something I could resist. The smell of sugar and chocolate hit me when I walked inside. My senses perked up and my skin seemed to tingle. Sue stood behind a wooden rail at a marble table, spreading out hot fudge. There was a small crowd gathered at the railing watching as she used her spatula to even out the gooey mixture on the slab. She saw me and gave me a wink while she explained what she was doing step-by-step in the process. Mia and Steph stood behind the candy case boxing up goodies for customers. I got in line and watched my stepdaughter work.

She was friendly and efficient. I could tell she was a hard worker. I wondered if Ben had ever been in and watched her. He'd be proud. I was proud. She was a young lady who still had mood swings and teen behavioral tendencies, but she was a good-hearted, sweet girl.

When I got to the front of the line, she shook her fudge cutter at me. "We don't need more sugar in the house."

"I know. I just want one piece. Maybe two. That's it."

"Well, I'm not allowed to refuse service, so what kind would you like?"

I placed my order for a piece of rocky road and a piece of walnut maple. She wrapped them up and I paid. "Is there anything you want me to bring you? Soapy has some hot apple cider."

"I'm fine. Steph and I are going to take a break as soon as her mom's done with that batch. I want to go up and see Dog Diggity."

"Monica would love it if you guys stopped in." I reached across the counter and gave her hand a squeeze. I resisted the urge to gush about my pride in her to save her embarrassment. The words would keep until later at home.

Next door, Brenda had her gothic horror novels out on display and her sister was in full fortune teller regalia at a separate, small table draped in black silk. Tarot cards and a crystal ball sat in front of her. She had a customer—a woman I'd never seen before, probably a tourist—enthralled in hearing her future.

I thought back to my own reading. Good gravy! She'd been right. She told me someone needed rescuing in a barn. I'd assumed she knew the story of how I had to go haul Roy out of the horse stable at the race track. But Good Luck Chuck was who needed rescuing from a barn!

"You look like you've seen a ghost," Brenda said.

"No. Not a ghost. A fortune teller."

"She has that effect on a few people."

"I didn't believe her, but she was right."

Brenda straightened a book on her table. "Well, I don't buy into that nonsense and chalk it up to coincidence."

"Coincidence," I repeated, mindlessly. "How long is she staying?"

"Why, do you want another reading?" she teased.

"No, I've had my fill. Just curious."

"She leaves tomorrow afternoon. I'll miss her. We hardly get to see each other anymore with our busy lives. Hers more than mine. I can always be found here between these dusty stacks of books."

"Don't try and make me jealous," I said. "That sounds like heaven to me."

"That reminds me." She rummaged around in a box under the table and brought forth a mystery novel. "I put this aside for you to read. I think you'll like it."

"*Festival Day Fatality*," I read.

"It's a great who-done-it. I've read it three times."

"Alright, thanks." I wasn't sure I was up for any more death just now, but maybe I'd pick it up in a few weeks.

The woman with Amelia got up and left the fortune telling table, fanning herself and looking like she knew more than she ever wanted to know. "Hello, Cameron," Amelia said. "Care to sit down?"

"Hi, Amelia. I was just on my way back to my table. Can't leave Johnna alone too long."

"No, I suppose not if you want to have anything left when you get back."

I smiled, unsure if what she knew about Johnna was from gossip or her supposed psychic ability.

"You found whoever was in need of rescue?" she asked.

"Yes. A dog, actually, and Johnna took him in."

"Oh, the companion I saw coming into her life. I'm very happy for them both. Should I say congratulations to your sister yet?"

"I don't think so. They just met not long ago. He lives in Ireland. She's not sure how it'll work when he goes back."

She gave me a mysterious grin. "When the time comes, tell her congratulations from me, will you?"

I nodded. Who did this lady think she was anyway? "I better get back. Nice seeing you both. Have a safe trip home, Amelia."

I waved as I walked away, eager to shake off the feeling of having someone seeing you from the inside out. Whether Amelia had some kind of special power or not, she was unnerving.

Nice, but unnerving.

∞

It was late afternoon, and the patrons had thinned a bit. Mia and Steph came running up to the Action Agency table. Mia had Liam tucked under her arm, and all I could see was his little white head. "Have you seen my dad?" she asked.

"No. Why? Is everything okay?"

"Yeah," she said, breathless, "everything's fine."

"What are you doing with Liam? Don't you have to go back to work soon?"

"Uh, yeah. I, um, I..."

"We have to get going," Steph said, dragging Mia into Dog Diggity by the arm.

"Those girls are up to something," Johnna said, not bothering to look up from her knitting.

"Umm hmm," Roy agreed, cocking his eyebrow at me.

"Well, whatever it is, I don't want to know about it." I set out the last few jars from the box under the table. We had one more box for the next day. If it turned out to be like today's sales, we'd be sitting pretty—literally, at new desks.

I heard a familiar deep bark from inside Dog Diggity. "That sounded just like Gus."

"How 'bout that," Roy said.

Johnna didn't say anything, which was very un-Johnna like. Something was up.

Soapy jogged up to the table. "I need you to come with me," he said.

"What happened?"

"Nothing happened. I just need you for a minute."

"We'll watch the table, Cameron Cripps-Hayman," Roy said, "you run along."

I didn't think it was possible to be more suspicious. "Okay." I stepped around the table and went with Soapy.

"Don't worry. It's nothing bad."

"What is it?"

"I can't tell you."

"This sounds sketchy to me."

He laughed. "Trust me, you'll enjoy it."

We stopped at the Soapy Savant, where Theresa was waiting in a lawn chair with two empty chairs beside her. "Take a seat," she said. "Have some more cider."

"What's going on? Why are you sitting here on the side of the road?"

"Just sit down, Cam, and stop asking questions."

So I sat. Soapy and Theresa chatted. I watched people continue to walk to vendors tables and then Anna was on a microphone. "Can I have your attention ladies and gentlemen? Please direct your eyes toward the gristmill for a Halloween treat."

Music began to play. Upbeat band music. I realized it was a real band. The high school's marching band. And then there they were, marching down the street in full uniform. It was a parade!

"Who organized this?" I asked Soapy.

"It was a coordinated effort, but Mia led the charge."

"Mia? Really?" Again, pride swelled in my chest. I'd grounded her from the pageant that Irene ended up canceling, and she'd gone out of her way to plan this and kept it a secret from me. The whole reason she was grounded to begin with was because she wanted to make me and Ben proud, wanted to be like Anna and Logan and help me figure out who killed Butch Landow.

Sometimes—most of the time—I didn't give her enough credit. She wanted what everyone wanted: to be noticed, appreciated, and loved. And she was. All of those things. But Ben and I needed to show it more. She was growing up and needed more than to be told how pretty she was.

We cheered as the band passed, blasting horns and beating drums. Behind them came the best part of all. The dog parade! Mia was out front walking Liam, who was dressed in a faux black leather biker jacket with a bandana around his head. A tattoo of a heart with MOM written inside was chalked in black on his tiny bottom. Mia had changed into cut off shorts and an old Harley Davidson t-shirt that

Ben had owned forever. Her hair was tied back with a bandana that matched Liam's.

"Look at them!" I said, laughing my head off, waving.

Next came Johnna and Chuck, who had a white knitted unicorn horn stuck to his head with elastic that went under his chin. Johnna had knitted him a brown saddle that tied around his middle and sat on his back. To top it all, Johnna was dressed like a fairy princess. My eyes couldn't behold so much pink glitter.

"Oh my," Soapy said next to me. "That's quite the costume."

"Johnna, you sparkle!" Theresa shouted.

Johnna waved her wand in our direction.

"Chuck for the win!" I heard Elaina shout from farther down the parade route.

Behind Johnna and Chuck, Quinn walked Conan, who was dressed like a prisoner in a striped jumpsuit. Quinn wore a police cap and tipped it in our direction as he walked by.

"Haul him away!" Soapy shouted.

More neighbors and people from town who I didn't know but recognized, strutted by with their dogs in matching costumes. There was Batman walking Superman, Darth Vader walking Princess Leia, and a litter of puppy ghosts being pulled in a wagon by a pre-teen vampire.

I never wanted it to end.

But it turned out that the end was the best part. Along came Ben with our pack of mutts. The twins, Mario and Luigi, wore the spaghetti and meatball costumes Mom had made. Mario kept jumping at Luigi and biting his meatballs. Gus and Brutus were skeletons, with white felt bone cut-outs strapped around their furry black legs and bodies with elastic. And Isobel was a wicked witch, which was a perfect costume for her personality. She growled and nipped at Gus and Brutus's tails.

Ben was dressed like a zombie.

"Its like the book!" I yelled to him.

He pointed to me, laughing. "You got it!"

In the book and the movie, the zombie main character had one mission: to capture the dog that he couldn't seem to capture. We figured it was some sort of metaphor for him trying to chase down everything he missed in life before he turned into a zombie. But Ben the Zombie had a whole pack of dogs, just like he had a whole pack of successes in life. His job, his friends and family, Mia, and me. If he were to ever turn into a zombie, he'd have no regrets.

Neither would I.

· Twenty-Two ·

O nce Ben passed by with our brood, the parade was over. "That was amazing," I said. I couldn't stop smiling. I had to be glowing.

"There's one more thing to come," Soapy said, holding out his hand to me.

I took it and he led me across the street to where Anna was standing with a wireless microphone. She handed it to Soapy, and he lifted it to speak. "And now, as Mayor of Metamora, it's my honor to crown the Canal Days Hero. This honor goes to the person who went above and beyond to put on a fantastic event for our town. I'm pleased to present to you, Cameron Cripps-Hayman."

I stood, stunned looking out at the applauding crowd. Anna handed me a scarecrow wearing a sash that said *Canal Days Hero*.

"You thought of this, didn't you?" I asked her.

She nodded. "How did you know?"

In answer, I hugged her. How could I not know? It was a gender-neutral award that was based on merit. It was what she believed in, and I couldn't be happier with the new recognition that someone would be awarded each year. "It's wonderful," I told her.

Soapy handed me the microphone. "Thank you," I said. "This is such a surprise. The parade, the costumes, this." I held out my scarecrow. "But I can't take the credit for something that so many people had a big part of planning. The Metamora Action Agency," I said, waving them forward, "and my daughter, Mia," I said, dropping the *step* from in front of *daughter* and hoping she wouldn't be offended. "And Soapy, of course."

They all took their acknowledgment in stride and hurried back to the sidelines to escape the spotlight. Thankfully for Johnna, because she was blinding in her sparkles, and Logan was sopping wet.

"And I want to say thanks to my Mom and my sister for being there for me during the tough days, and to my … my Ben, for everything, always."

I handed the mic back to Soapy and escaped with my scarecrow.

"Did you love it?" Mia asked, rushing up to me.

"More than I've ever loved anything in my life," I said, kissing the top of Liam's head. "This was the best surprise I've ever gotten, Mia. Thank you. I'll never forget it." I leaned in and kissed her forehead. "You're a sweet, loving girl."

I'd never seen her smile bigger. "I'm off work," she said. "I just said I was on break to keep this a secret."

"I guess that's okay. One small twist of the truth to not ruin a special surprise."

Ben was attempting to make his way to us, but Mario and Luigi kept chasing each other's meatballs around his legs, making Isobel snarl, which made Brutus bark. Gus was trying to pull away to beg pets from strangers.

"We better save him," I said.

Mia took Isobel, and I took the twins, leaving Ben with Brutus and Gus. "Zombie eat dogs for breakfast," Ben said, groaning and shuffling his feet. "Taste like chicken."

"Gross!" Mia squealed.

He laughed and gave her ponytail a playful tug. "We're supposed to all meet back at Dog Diggity," he said.

I yanked Mario away from Luigi as we set off. "Monica has to be elated with how well today went."

"She definitely seemed happy," he said. "Cass couldn't keep the shelves stocked. Monica was lucky to have her help in there today."

"I'm so glad she could help out, too, since we thought of selling honey at the last minute and I couldn't."

"I heard about the church."

I shrugged. "I never liked working in that smelly basement anyway. We'll find somewhere better."

"Ben!" Irene called from the Daughters of Metamora booth. "You were wonderful!"

"Thanks, Mom," he said.

"You, too, Cameron," she said, like she had a mouth full of lemons.

"Thank you, Irene," I said back, as sweet as pie.

Ben laughed and shook his head. "Someday the two of you will get along."

"No, we won't."

"No, you won't," he agreed, laughing even harder.

We got to Dog Diggity and the closed sign was in the window. The sun was setting, so I guessed it was around seven in the evening. Monica must've been out of stock.

The three of us clambered inside with our dogs. Mom was there with Carl, and Andy and Cass. Quinn was behind the counter with Monica, helping her close up shop for the day.

"So?" I said, resting my elbows on the sales counter. "How was your first day in business?"

Frazzled, Monica beamed with joy. "I couldn't have wished for any better," she said. "But there is something." Her eyes turned to Quinn.

He took her hand and they walked out from behind the counter. "We have an announcement," he said.

My heart seized. What was this?

"As you all know, my home is in Ireland. I came here to help train Brutus. I had no plans on meeting someone and beginning a relationship. But here we are," he said, putting an arm around Monica. "I have an opportunity to start a new business, and Monica has agreed to help me with it. We'll help each other."

"In Ireland?" Mom asked, putting a hand to her chest.

"No, Mom," Monica said. "He's staying here."

"I bought Bantum Kennel, and I'm turning it into a dog training facility. So I'll be right beyont," he said waving a hand in the general direction of Connersville.

"Oh, how wonderful," Mom clasped her hands together. "We were so worried about Monica losing you."

"Mom," Monica said, a warning tone in her voice.

"Welcome to the neighborhood," I said, clapping Quinn on the back. "Or close enough. Do I get a multi-dog discount?"

He chuckled. "We'll think on it."

Ben shook his hand. I could tell he was glad Quinn was staying, they'd become good friends.

My twin Italian stallions barked up a storm and chased each other around the store. "I better get these guys out of here before they tear the place apart."

Ben, Mia, and I said goodbye to everyone and went on our way. The sun was down and only a pink haze remained in the sky. "Red sky at night, sailors delight," I said.

"Good," Ben said, "I've had enough rain to last a lifetime."

As we neared the bridge over the canal, Spook darted out from nowhere, hissing at the dogs and racing across. The twins went ballistic and took off after the cat. I tried to hold them back, but they're like little bulls packed with the muscles of Hulk. Gus and Brutus were right behind, doing their best to get away from Ben. He yelled, "Brutus, heel!" but with his old partner in crime, Gus, at his side, Brutus wasn't as dignified as he was in Conan's presence. The commands went out the window.

Spook jumped off the bridge onto the bank and skittered up a tree. My dogs dashed around the end of the bridge, pulling me into the edge of the railing, and hightailed it down the bank in search of their prey. "He's up in the tree, you ding-dongs!" I shouted.

That's when Metamora Mike showed up, splashing down in the canal. It was quite the attention-getting landing. The twins didn't know what to do. Cat or duck? Cat or duck? In the end, they decided both. One went one way, the other went the other, and I was stuck in the middle of their tug-of-war.

The bank wasn't yet dried out from the flood. My foot slipped, and I fought to keep my balance. But down I went, right into the water.

Oh, good gravy. What a way to end Canal Days.

∞

The sun was shining brightly, drying the grass and warming the air. My bees were busy buzzing in their hive. Old Dan said to sing to them. Well, singing wasn't going to happen, but I did have another musical talent, if I did say so myself.

I sat in a lawn chair beside the bee box in the front yard and opened my clarinet case. Certainly, if bees liked music they weren't so picky as to the type. "I know 'Hot Cross Buns' and most of 'Mary Had A Little Lamb,'" I told them as I assembled my instrument. "Don't sting me if my reed squeaks, I'm new at this."

After opening my music book and laying it by my feet, I sat on the edge of my chair and lifted the clarinet to my lips. Taking a deep breath, I placed my fingers in the B position and then blew into the horn. An ear-splitting squeal was the only noise I managed to make. A rumble of outraged buzzing emitted from the hive, and the dogs howled and barked in the backyard.

"Okay, okay," I said to myself and the bees, "calm down. That was just a practice note. I blew too hard. Let's try again."

More slowly this time, I eased air past the reed. A note rang out clear as a bell. "I did it!"

Soon, I was honking right through the beginning. *Hot cross buns! Hot cross buns!*

The phone began to ring inside the house. "I'll be right back," I told my winged audience, and hustled up the porch steps and through the door. "Hello?" I said, answering the cordless phone.

"Stop that infernal racket!" Fiona cried. "I'll continue to give you lessons, but you can't play in public until I say you're ready. We can hear you over the train!"

"Train?" I glanced out my front window. "Huh, what do you know. I didn't hear it pull into the station either."

"Exactly my point. Be here tomorrow morning at nine," she said, and hung up.

"She doesn't know what she's talking about," I told Spook, who'd appeared out of nowhere to wrap his tail around my shins. "I'm doing very well for a beginner."

Mia traipsed down the stairs rolling her eyes and sighing dramatically. "Steph just sent me a text message asking if there was a dying goat in our yard. You're so embarrassing."

Ben pulled into the driveway in Metamora One, got out, and hoofed it to the door double-speed. "I got a complaint of disrupting the peace from this address," he said, coming through the door.

"It was her and that thing," Mia said, pointing at me and my clarinet.

Soapy followed Ben inside. "As the mayor of this town—"

"I'm done, okay?" I said, shoving the clarinet into Ben's hands. "Good gravy! A woman can't even practice the clarinet in her own yard around here without it becoming a police matter!"

"Why were you playing in the front yard?" Ben asked.

"If you must know, Old Dan told me I had to sing to the bees. You know me and singing don't mix. I thought I'd try to play for them instead."

"Oh. Right," Ben said. "Good call. Don't sing to them unless you want them to fly away for their lives."

I shot him a dirty glare.

"You're supposed talk to them, not sing to them," Soapy said. "My mother used to keep bees. Every evening after dinner she'd sit beside their hive with her embroidery and tell them the day's gossip. She always said if you didn't keep the queen up to date on the town happenings she'd get offended and they'd swarm."

"Really?" I said. "I just have to talk to them? I can do that."

"Yes, you can," Ben said. "Sometimes I don't think you'll ever keep your nose out of my business, so go tell them all about Butch Landow and how you almost got yourself killed."

"Someone's still a little salty," Mia said, traipsing back up the stairs.

"I had a concussion, that's all," I told him. "Don't make it a bigger deal than it was."

"I'll wait in the truck," Soapy said, clearly uncomfortable being at the scene of a budding domestic dispute. "Cam, the next town event isn't until after the new year, so you just rest up."

When he'd walked out onto the porch and pulled the door shut behind him, Ben set the clarinet on the hall table and took my hand. "I'm serious, Cam. Just because you're still married to a police officer and you somehow have made a habit of stumbling across recently deceased townspeople, you don't have the training or authority to get involved in these cases. When you were lying unconscious—"

"I fell down the hill. I was fine."

"Maybe so, but that makes the second time I've shown up on a scene to arrest a murderer to find that you just narrowly escaped with your own life. There can't be a next time."

"Well, I'm not planning on finding another dead person, Ben, so you can stop worrying."

He sighed his annoyed, frustrated, resigned sigh reserved just for me, and nodded. "We're still on for our Wednesday movie this week?"

"We better be. You owe me pizza afterward, too, for doing your job for you." I knew my bad joke was pushing him too far as soon as it was out of my mouth. "I'm just kidding," I said quickly.

Ben shook his head. "I guess I can spring for pizza and peanut M&M's since you solved the case. And it will be your last."

After he left, I resumed my spot in the lawn chair beside the beehive. "Well, what can I tell you, Queenie?" I settled back and gazed up at the streaky white clouds floating by in the bright blue sky. "It all started with polka dots. I knew they were deadly."

*B*one-shaped cookie cutters are sold at many craft stores, but any shape will work. Vary the size of the treats based on your own fur friends! Store your biscuits in an air-tight container, or freeze for long-term storage. *Please be aware of any dietary restrictions your dog has prior to giving them human food.*

DOGS DIG LEFTOVERS

2½ cups flour (regular, whole wheat, or oats)

1 tsp. salt

1 egg

¼ cup beef or chicken stock

¼ cup hot water

1 tbsp. peas

1 tbsp. finely chopped carrots

1 tbsp. finely shredded beef, cooked
  (cooked hamburger is a good replacement)

Preheat oven to 350 degrees. Mix all ingredients, kneading until dough forms a ball. Roll dough to ½-inch thickness. Slice or cut with bone-shaped cookie cutter. Move biscuits to lightly greased cookie sheet and bake for 30 minutes.

Our Dog Diggity taste testers also approve of chicken instead of beef!

DOGS DIG ITALIAN BISCUITS

2½ cups flour (regular, whole wheat, or oats)
1 tsp. salt
1 egg
¼ cup beef or chicken stock
¼ cup hot water
1 tbsp. finely shredded fresh basil
½ cup ricotta cheese

Preheat oven to 350 degrees. Mix all ingredients, kneading until dough forms a ball. Roll dough to ½-inch thickness. Slice or cut with bone-shaped cookie cutter. Move biscuits to lightly greased cookie sheet and bake for 30 minutes.

Dog Diggity taste testers also love cottage cheese and oregano!

DOGS DIG HONEY BONES

2½ cups flour (regular, whole wheat, or oats)
1 tsp. salt
1 egg
½ cup hot water
½ cup of raw, local honey (or honey from your grocery store)

Preheat oven to 350 degrees. Mix all ingredients, kneading until dough forms a ball. Roll dough to ½-inch thickness. Slice or cut with bone-shaped cookie cutter. Move biscuits to lightly greased cookie sheet and bake for 30 minutes.

Dog Diggity taste testers also love it when we add peanut butter and mashed bananas to this recipe!

ABOUT THE AUTHOR

Jamie M. Blair (Ohio) is the *New York Times* bestselling author of young adult and romance books, including *Leap of Faith* (Simon & Schuster, 2013) and *Lost to Me* (2014). You can visit her online at www.JamieBlairAuthor.com.

WWW.MIDNIGHTINKBOOKS.COM

From the gritty streets of New York City to sacred tombs in the Middle East, it's always midnight somewhere. Join us online at any hour for fresh new voices in mystery fiction.

At midnightinkbooks.com you'll also find our author blog, new and upcoming books, events, book club questions, excerpts, mystery resources, and more.

MIDNIGHT INK ORDERING INFORMATION

 ### Order Online:
- Visit our website www.midnightinkbooks.com, select your books, and order them on our secure server.

 ### Order by Phone:
- Call toll-free within the U.S. and Canada at 1-888-NITE-INK (1-888-648-3465)
- We accept VISA, MasterCard, American Express and Discover

 ### Order by Mail:
Send the full price of your order (MN residents add 6.875% sales tax) in U.S. funds, plus postage & handling to:

> Midnight Ink
> 2143 Wooddale Drive
> Woodbury, MN 55125-2989

Postage & Handling:
Standard (U.S. & Canada). If your order is:
> $30.00 and under, add $4.00
> $30.01 and over, FREE STANDARD SHIPPING

International Orders:
> $16.00 for one book plus $3.00 for each additional book

Orders are processed within 12 business days. Please allow for normal shipping time.
Postage and handling rates subject to change.

20x